R.L. PEREZ

SERPENT & FLAME

AN IVY & BONE NOVEL

WILLOW
HAVEN
PRESS

CHAPTER ONE

MARINA SAT ON THE BRIDGE THAT SPANNED THE Snake River, her feet dangling over the edge as she stared into the roiling depths below. This was one of the few places where her mind—and the raging magic within her—could be quieted. The sound of rushing waters surrounded her, almost drowning out the incessant pull of the fire burning within her.

Almost.

She could never fully find peace. Not here. Not ever. But she could certainly come close. Sometimes the overwhelming roar of the river did the trick. Otherwise it was utter and perfect silence she craved.

And then, of course, there was her favorite remedy: making love to attractive young men. The sheer ecstasy of it helped fill her senses with other intense emotions, momentarily blocking out the pain of her magic. But men were few and far between in a witch coven, and women didn't have the same appeal to Marina, so that wasn't always a viable option.

"I thought I might find you here."

Marina looked up and smiled in spite of the turmoil in her mind. Remy, her mother, stood before her, adorned in an aqua blue gown that matched the river perfectly. A diadem rested in her hair with gleaming aquamarine stones, marking her as the coven leader.

"You aren't dressed," Remy observed, sweeping her long chestnut braid over one shoulder so she could sit on the edge with her daughter. Her legs didn't hang as low as Marina's; on a good day, Marina could dip her toes in and feel the cool current rush over her. Not many in the coven were tall enough to manage it.

"It's worse today." Marina rubbed her temples with a sigh.

Remy touched her shoulder. "I can ask Giselle to make you another tonic."

Marina suppressed a wince. Giselle's tonics didn't always help, and they tasted like fish shit. More often than not, Marina preferred to brave her pains alone, without having that foul taste in her mouth.

"I know it's hard, love," Remy said softly. "But today is important."

Marina nodded. She knew this. It didn't stop the

pain, though. Every day she suppressed her fire magic, it only scorched her insides, threatening to consume her entirely. "It's been years, Mama. How much longer will it take for them to accept me as one of their own?"

Remy offered a sad smile. "There is a delicate balance to covens. Bringing in an outsider is *never* done. We are breaking generations of tradition by letting you in. Try to understand what that means for everyone."

Yes, consider the coven, Marina thought bitterly. *Think of them and how hard it is. Not how hard it is for* me. *No one seems to care about that.*

Remy had found Marina as a toddler, wandering aimlessly in the woods, her hands alight with flame. No one knew who or where Marina's parents were. But it was obvious she was a fire witch.

Remy was within her right to banish or execute Marina on the spot. In Sodara, fire witches were hunted and destroyed because of their volatile power. If left unchecked, these witches had the power to slaughter an entire village with a single flame from their finger.

So, yes, Remy was correct. It *was* unheard of for a coven of water witches to take in an outsider. Especially an outsider whose very existence was a crime. Remy had given her the name Marina, after the sea. For years, Marina had worked, toiling day after day to help the coven and improve the lives of the witches, desperate to prove herself, to be accepted, to be *loved.*

In the end, though, it was only Remy who loved her. But perhaps that was enough. Not everyone was so lucky, after all. And if Remy wasn't the coven leader, Marina was certain she would have been cast out ages ago.

"I love this river," Remy said absently, her gaze fixed on the current below them. "It's a reminder that magic is all around us. It lives in the water at our feet. It lives in the rivers and the seas." She looked at Marina with fondness in her eyes. "I wish I could remain out here with you, but I can't stay long."

With a sigh, Marina leaned her head on her mother's shoulder. "I know. I'll be along soon. I just needed a quiet moment before all the chaos."

Tonight was Litha, the summer solstice. Their coven always celebrated with a masquerade festival full of music, dancing, and an excess of food and spirits. Generally, Marina enjoyed the Litha celebration. In the beginning, it was a sacred ceremony, and it was important for her to be present to show her support of the coven. But after that, when the merriment began, it was an opportunity for her to mask her identity and simply *exist*. To enjoy revelry and merriment without fear of being judged or despised, for once. Once the other witches had consumed enough alcohol, none of them cared that Marina was a despised fire witch, even if they *could* recognize her behind the mask.

Remy kissed her cheek lightly. "Don't take too long, Mare."

Marina nodded, closing her eyes as her mother rose and strode down the bridge, her sandals slapping lightly against the wooden surface. Soon, it was only the sound of the river, and the constant churning of the flames burning just under her skin. Rising, rising, rising, like a phoenix from the ashes. Her chest was on fire. Her blood was boiling. Everything was hot; far too hot. She tried to focus on the soothing rhythm of the lapping water, but all she saw in her mind was a deadly inferno.

It was getting worse. Remy and Marina tried to ignore it, but the evidence was there. Sometimes Marina would find her hands aglow with sparks she couldn't put out. Other times, Remy swore Marina's usually green eyes had flashed a bright amber, the color of liquid flame.

It was only a matter of time before her powers were too explosive to contain.

When that moment came, Marina vowed she would flee. She wouldn't endanger this coven. They may not have fully accepted her, but they had given refuge to her for almost twenty years. And that was an extraordinary blessing Marina would never forget. She couldn't risk unleashing her power on them.

She wrung her hands together on her lap, trying to swallow past the burning ache in her throat. This was the third day this week she couldn't function because of the pain. "This can't go on," she whispered, her voice drowned out by the sound of the river. "I must leave. And soon. Before someone gets hurt."

Remy would object, of course, claiming there were ways to tame her magic, to soothe her pain. But all the remedies would only be temporary. Marina's magic was too powerful to be squashed down for long. She wasn't a water witch, no matter how much she pretended to be. Eventually, she would have to leave. Remy would accept this. In time.

With a shuddering breath, Marina stood, staring into the river's depths for a moment longer before crossing the bridge and returning to her house.

A celebration awaited her. And it would be her last one.

The sounds of laughter and idle chatter echoed in the forest as Marina adjusted the strap of her dress, feeling naked with so little fabric covering her. She wore a gown made of turquoise satin that brought out the green in her eyes and clung to her body, though not uncomfortably. The fabric was flexible, allowing her to move freely without her skirts getting in the way. The dress only fell to her knees, swishing with each step. It hung on one shoulder, leaving the other bare, exposing the pale skin she was often embarrassed by. Most water witches had tan complexions, as they often dwelled outside by the water. But no matter how much time she spent in the sun, Marina's pale skin never darkened, as if she were cursed to always be different despite her best efforts.

And it was ironic because on the inside, Marina was always burning. That her skin should be bone-white was Fate's cruel joke.

But soon it would be dusk, and no one would notice the pallor of her skin or the gleam of her eyes. Her black hair would blend in with the browns of those around her, and anyone who might pay attention to such details would be too intoxicated to care. She had her peacock mask tied at her throat, ready to don it as soon as the sacred ceremony had ended. Already, she could sense the other witches watching her, some in curiosity and others with open hostility.

Marina kept her head held high, her gaze fixed straight ahead.

She joined the witches gathering in the sacred stone circle, placing herself between Remy and Giselle, who offered a gentle smile. Giselle was one of the few witches who always treated Marina with kindness. Marina took her hand and returned the smile.

"Blessed be," said Nadia, the high priestess, who

stood at the front of the circle. "Today marks the pinnacle of the sun's great power. Today we give thanks to the light and to all Tethys has bestowed upon us. Our waters flow freely because of her benevolence."

"Blessed be the Goddess," Marina murmured along with the witches next to her.

"We offer our bodies and our blood to better serve the river Goddess." Nadia raised a blade and pressed the tip into her pointer finger. A bead of blood welled from the wound and dripped into the chalice in her other hand. She passed the chalice to the witches in the circle. One by one, they pressed blades to their flesh and allowed their blood to join the others' in the goblet.

Marina fidgeted as the goblet came closer to her. The last time she'd participated in this ceremony, her blood had accidentally set fire to the chalice... and almost the entire forest.

What was worse? Abstaining from a sacred rite and risking the wrath of her coven, or potentially endangering them with her volatile blood?

When the chalice reached her, Marina swallowed hard. Remy watched her expectantly and offered a sure nod, urging her onward.

All right, Marina thought with a deep breath. *Let's see what happens.* She took the blade from Remy's hand and pressed it into her littlest finger. As the blood welled, she crammed her eyes shut, gritting her teeth as she put all of her effort into subduing her magic, quenching the roaring within her veins. She focused on the noises around her—the babbling river in the distance, the chirping of birds and insects, the whisper of the wind...

As she opened her eyes, she let her blood fall into the chalice. For one blessed moment, there was nothing but silence in her mind, the echoes of the forest a soothing balm to her pain. She stared at the collection of blood in the goblet, holding her breath, waiting...

The chalice moved on to Giselle, who seemed to slice herself rather quickly, as if she, too, was worried Marina's blood would cause a reaction. Marina shot her a grateful smile, finally releasing her breath as the chalice continued around the circle.

When the ceremony was finished, each witch bowed her head and whispered, "Blessed be the Goddess." Nadia walked around the circle, pressing her thumb to each witch's forehead, symbolizing the awakening of the third eye. She stiffened when she reached Marina, her nose wrinkling as if her fire magic smelled foul. Marina endured this as she always did, with a pleasant smile on her face, thanking Nadia after she touched her forehead.

That bitch never liked Marina. But that was fine. Marina didn't care much for her, either.

When Nadia was finished, she dismissed the coven, encouraging them to enjoy the festivities. Marina turned to leave, but Remy caught her in a tight embrace first.

"I'm so proud of you," she whispered against her hair, clutching her firmly.

"For not setting the forest on fire?" Marina said with a chuckle.

Remy withdrew and tucked a stray strand of raven-black hair behind Marina's ear. "For enduring it with a smile. And for doing your part. You offer so much and get so little in return, Mare. Someday the Goddess will bless you for it."

Marina highly doubted this, but she couldn't begrudge her mother's faith. Instead, she nodded and kissed Remy's cheek. "Will you stay for the festival?"

Remy sighed and shook her head. "I may grab a sweet treat or two, but I am already too fatigued. Besides, Giselle needs my help. A healer's hands are never idle."

As the most powerful witch in the coven, Remy was constantly called upon to use her powers and assist those who needed help. A bout of fever had been spreading through the coven as of late, leaving Giselle swamped with healing and creating tonics. Remy had been working alongside her, tiring endlessly to bring healing to those who had been afflicted.

Marina squeezed Remy's hands. "You do too much."

Remy shook her head. "I am blessed and must share that blessing with others. It's the way of our people."

"Get some rest, then," Marina said. "I will just have to have twice as much fun to make up for your absence."

Remy grinned. "I hope you do."

Marina watched her mother's lithe, elegant figure stride down the forest path and out of sight. With a heavy sigh, she donned her mask and followed the crowd away from the sacred stone circle and toward the festivities.

Marina walked the forest path up the hill until it opened to a wide trail lined with peddlers' carts and stands. Litha was an opportunity for merchants to come from afar and sell their wares, or join in the merriment like everyone else. She always loved seeing new things, tasting new foods, and meeting foreigners.

She adjusted her peacock mask, its feathers tickling her forehead, as she made her way through the crowd. A small smile played at her lips, her gaze roving over those haggling with vendors, purchasing food, or twirling to the sound of the music pouring from the pavilion. Someone grabbed her arm and spun her, laughing, the smell of alcohol on their breath. Marina allowed herself to be swept up into the dance, her arms finding her partner's waist—a shorter woman with curly brown hair and a wide, infectious smile. Brenna, the coven apothecary. Marina recognized her easily, though Brenna didn't seem to know who she was.

No matter. Marina flashed her a grin and continued with their dance until Brenna had moved on to another partner.

From there, it was easy for Marina to lose herself in the festivities. She purchased sticky buns and a glass of rose wine, though she was careful not to drink too much. With her powers, she could never be too careful. Gradually, she made her way to the pavilion to watch the crowd dance together, their steps synchronized and their laughter echoing. A young man touched Marina's elbow, his eyes glinting from underneath his raven mask, and asked for a dance.

Marina obliged, enjoying the warm embrace of the man's arms winding around her. There were few men in their coven, as most witch abilities only passed to females. But Litha brought all manner of people from the outlying villages, and Marina was grateful for the escape, for the chance to laugh and flirt and pretend she was someone else. It was a sweet release, to be around people who didn't know her or fear her. She reveled in it.

And, if she was lucky, the night would end with a satisfying dalliance that would cool and quiet her mind for one blessed night. She only had to find the right partner, but judging by the looks of it, there were many men here fit for the task.

She danced with three more men before she had to rest, the fire churning in her belly so intensely she almost couldn't see straight. Stumbling, she made her way out the pavilion and toward the temple perched on the hill. Ordinarily, it was a place of worship, a place for sacred things. No one would be there now, and what Marina needed most was the quiet. She would return when the pain had subsided and continue her search for a bedmate for the night.

Gasping for breath after climbing the hill, Marina burst inside, and darkness washed over her. She lit a single torch against the wall, which highlighted the statue of Tethys, the river goddess who watched over them. With a sigh, she leaned her head against the wall, relishing the feel of the cool marble against her skin.

"I hope I'm not intruding," said a deep voice.

Marina jumped, her pulse skittering as she scanned her surroundings. A shadow peeled away from the wall, coming into view—a man wearing all black, save for the crimson mask covering his face.

Marina pressed a hand to her chest, trying to calm her racing heart. "I—I thought I was alone in here. Forgive me. I'll leave you to your prayers."

She turned away, but the man started laughing. "Prayers? Oh, I think not. No, I only came for a moment of peace and quiet. Chaos and revelry are wonderful in small doses, but should I partake of too much, my mind becomes an inescapable storm." He shook his head. "But enough about me. If *you* are here to worship, I will, of course, leave you."

"I confess I'm not. I, too, came to escape." She cocked

her head at him. "You aren't from around here, are you?"

The man flashed a wide grin as he drew closer. His face was lined with a faint amount of facial hair, making him look older than Marina originally thought. His voice was deep, but still youthful. He was likely only twenty or so, if she had to hazard a guess. "No, I'm from... much farther than most of the guests here. I'm merely passing through on my way back home."

"And where is home?"

Half his mouth quirked upward in a coy smile. "Ah, I thought the point of this little festival was to be anonymous. If I give away too many details, that would take out all the fun."

Marina found herself smiling because she agreed with this. Being in disguise, being unrecognizable, *was* the most alluring part of Litha. For all he knew, *she* could be a stranger passing through. He would have no way of knowing she belonged to this coven.

Or rather, *didn't* belong.

Feeling bold, Marina drew closer until they stood only a breath apart. She was tall, but he still towered over her, his frame large and impressive. A soldier perhaps? Her mouth went dry as she glanced over the bulk of his arms straining against his dark shirt. Goddess, the muscles he must have...

"I like that look," he murmured, his voice a soft caress.

She suppressed a shiver. "What look?"

"That look of hunger. And desire."

Marina laughed again, but it was light and a bit breathless. She *had* had her fair share of lovers. Mostly during Lithia, where anything was possible and there were no consequences. She never saw her lovers again, but that was part of the game. The thrill of it all.

"Why are you really here?" Marina asked, looking up into his eyes. They were an astonishing silver, glowing like the light of the moon. "Are you *truly* here for peace and quiet, or are you nothing more than a sly fox lying in wait for an unsuspecting maiden to stumble into your den?"

A low chuckle rumbled in his throat. "And are you that unsuspecting maiden? From that look you just gave me, I'd hardly consider you innocent."

"You didn't answer my question, Fox."

"I'm well aware, Jay."

"Jay?" Marina laughed. "What is that?"

The man gestured to her mask. "A blue jay, yes?"

"No. It's a peacock. Have you never seen one before?"

"I confess I haven't. Where I'm from, we don't have the luxury of such... beautiful creatures." His eyes gleamed as they roved over Marina's body.

Her insides heated from that look. Goddess, she

loved this, toying with men, pretending she was someone else, someone attractive. If he truly knew she was a fire witch, would he even look twice at her? He wasn't from here, and she couldn't sense a powerful aura of magic around him. He *could* be a witch, but if he was, he was no river witch. She knew their scent well.

"Perhaps it is only the costume you find beautiful," Marina challenged. "After all, my face is covered. For all you know, I could be a hideous hag beneath this." She pointed to her mask.

His gleam turned lethal as he approached her. "Then, perhaps we should remove your costume... and see what lies underneath." He lifted a hand as if to touch her, his knuckles just barely brushing the skin of her arm, before he withdrew it, his eyes conflicted.

Marina wasn't sure if she was relieved or disappointed. She lifted her chin. "Is that really what you want, Fox? You seem uncertain."

The man's jaw tensed, and he dropped his hand. "It is. But, unfortunately, it is not what I came here for."

"Ah, yes. You came here to escape. Perhaps you and I have different ideas of what that means."

He smiled, and it made him seem more relaxed. More at ease. "There are... rules I must follow. As alluring as you are, Jay, I fear the repercussions if I break those rules."

"Rules?" Marina wrinkled her nose. "This is Litha—

the one night we are allowed to break all rules."

He laughed. "Maybe for you. But I answer to a higher power."

"Higher than Tethys?"

"Yes."

Marina's face slackened in surprise. She had been teasing; she hadn't *really* thought this man before her answered to a deity. But then again, if he was a different kind of witch, perhaps there was another god or goddess he worshipped. One with stricter rules than Tethys. She crossed her arms and leaned against the cold stone wall. Inside her skin, her fire continued raging, but the distraction of bantering with this man kept it at bay, along with the chilled air in the temple.

"What exact rules must you follow, wicked fox?" Marina asked.

"I can only remain here for a short time before I am... summoned back home."

Marina nodded. "All right. That's easy to work around. What else?"

"I cannot consort with mortals. Or witches."

Marina laughed. "Mortals? So you are immortal, then?"

"In a sense. Let us say that I am not fully human."

Marina frowned in contemplation. This was unusual, but not unheard of. There were many species of halflings. She was a witch, after all, and could hardly be considered an average human herself. "Ah. Well, I'm afraid it's too late for you there. With that rule already broken, there isn't much else you can do."

The man lifted one shoulder. "Perhaps. But I have only thus far interacted with mortals and witches in passing. A small grievance like that is easy to cover up. But..." He inched closer to her, and her skin warmed from his proximity. "If I were to stay longer.... go deeper... push *harder*..." He drew out each word, eliciting a shuddering groan from Marina's chest. "...in the mortal world, well, it would be much harder to cover that up."

Mortal world. Was he not from the Realm of Gaia then?

This man was a mystery she wanted to unravel. Piece by piece.

She inched closer until her chest brushed against his as she peered up at him through her mask. "So, what will your choice be, Fox? Will you have me here and now, and grant us both the escape we desire? Or will you adhere to your rules and run back home only to feel... unsatisfied?"

This time, he was the one to groan, the sound somewhere between a growl and a sigh. He lifted his hand again, allowing his fingertips to brush against the bare skin of her arm. Marina closed her eyes, relishing that cool, gentle touch that seemed to soothe the roaring inferno inside her.

"You don't know me," he murmured. "And I don't know you."

"Doesn't that make this more exciting?" Marina breathed.

He leaned in, his mouth hovering over hers. Marina held still, waiting for him to close the distance between them. He hesitated for only a moment before sealing her lips with his. He tasted cool against the heat of her own body, and a tingle of awareness spread over her. His mouth moved more urgently as her tongue coaxed him onward, sliding between his lips and tasting him fully. He tasted like mint and oak and the hint of something sweet like caramel. Perhaps he'd enjoyed the sticky buns just like she had.

A feverish need spread through Marina, and she was lost after that. Her hands were against his chest, tugging his collar closer, her arms rising to wind around his neck and twine in his thick, dark hair. His hands found her waist, lining her hips with his. Together, they staggered until her back met the cold stone wall. He ground against her, his arousal pressed to her. She could feel every hard inch of him, and Goddess, it was glorious.

His lips moved to her neck, pressing soft kisses against her tender skin. He traveled lower, his mouth gliding along her collarbone and even lower, his tongue tracing circles just above her breasts. Marina gasped, fisting his hair as a riot of desire bolted through her. His hand slid under the strap of her dress before shifting it to the side, exposing her other shoulder and sliding it down, down, down. Her breathing turned ragged as the dress fell down to her waist, baring her breasts to him. He gazed at them with hunger in his eyes.

"Beautiful indeed," he whispered before lowering his mouth to her left breast, sucking and nipping, his teeth tugging gently against her peaked nipple.

"Goddess!" Marina moaned, writhing against him, her body aflame with a new kind of kindling, something that quenched her magic and ignited a carnal, sensuous desire. She yearned for that escape, for that peace, for the quiet of her mind and body where nothing existed but the flesh and touch of a man, the throes of pleasure and passion.

She tugged at his trousers, slipping her hand underneath and gripping his arousal firmly, running her hand up and down its length.

He slammed his hands into the wall behind her with a roar, grinding more fervently against her. With one swift movement, she lowered his trousers, admiring every beautiful inch of him. He kept one hand braced on the wall behind her and used the other to bunch her skirts higher. His fingers rose up her thigh, stroking and teasing as he drew closer to her center. When he reached the moisture collecting between her legs, his voice rumbled with satisfaction.

"Mmm, I make you wet, don't I?"

Marina ground against his hand, demanding more, but he only smirked. "How much wetter can I make you before you lose your mind?"

A small whimper rose up her throat. She swallowed it down and forced a steady voice as she said, "If it's torment you want, Fox, I can more than deliver."

He flashed a wicked grin. "Don't hold back."

Her hand grasped him fully again, her finger teasing its tip. He swore, his voice a low hiss, as he leaned in and caught her shoulder between his teeth. The sharpness of his bite sent a delightful sizzle through Marina's body, only fueling her arousal.

"How long will you make us both wait?" Marina gasped as his hand covered her breast again. She tugged more firmly against his length, dragging it closer to her. Her sex ached, throbbing with a painful longing that she couldn't ignore. "Give me my escape, Fox. And I'll give you yours."

A deep growl built in his throat as his arms grew taut around her, caging her in. She met his darkened gaze, challenging him, her chest heaving with her shallow breaths. She lifted one leg, wrapping it around his middle and rubbing her center directly against him.

His restraint snapped. His hands cupped her rear,

hitching the other leg up so she straddled him, her back still against the wall. He leaned in, his breath tickling her ear. "Try not to scream." His teeth pulled on her earlobe, and she shuddered, just as he buried himself deep inside her.

She cried out, trying to stifle the volume of her voice as he filled her completely. Goddess, the length of him, the way it glided inside her, farther, farther, *deeper...* Stars burst in her vision, her blood boiling and her skin melting from the sheer perfection of it. He withdrew, only to plunge into her again. She threw her head back against the wall, closing her eyes, her mouth open in rapture. His fingers traced her inner thigh as he found a rhythm, pounding into her again and again, her back ramming into the wall over and over. But the pain was intoxicating to her, only adding to the flood of sensations that drowned her. Her hands found his ass, pressing it fully against her, urging him to go harder, faster.

He obliged, ramming into her, a feral, animal sound rumbling from within him. She couldn't stop her moans of delight, her voice making strangled sounds she didn't recognize. Her legs clenched around him as the coiled tension inside her tightened, mounting higher and higher. Her skin burned. Her insides spiraled. She couldn't take it anymore. She needed release, *now.* Goddess, she was so close, so close....

He seemed to sense she was on the precipice. He

leaned in, scraping his teeth along her throat while his other hand pinched her nipple, twisting it until she screamed. Her climax tore through her, vicious and merciless. Heat and pain and the most intense pleasure she'd ever known washed over her, bringing a staggering sensation of hot and cold rippling over her skin and numbing her bones. Soon after, he roared with his own release, pressing hard, and whispering, "Oh gods... Oh *gods*..." Over and over.

When the air settled and Marina's breathing gradually returned to normal, she remained pinned against the wall with him inside her, his face buried in her neck.

"It's never been like that before," he groaned, his voice muffled against her. "Not for me."

Marina shook her head, but she was unable to speak. Her throat was raw from her screams, but she agreed. It had *never* been like that for her. Never had she been so fully satisfied, left so raw and brutally ravaged by a man's body. Ordinarily, she was in charge, showing men how rough she liked it, but none of them could deliver the way she wanted.

Not until *him*. This fox she would likely never see again.

Slowly, he lowered her to the ground. Her legs were throbbing, and when he withdrew completely from her, a gaping emptiness took his place.

I'll never feel that fulfilled again, Marina thought.

The man tugged his trousers back into place and adjusted his mask, which had kept his face covered the entire time. Marina was slightly disappointed by this; perhaps if she knew his face she would be able to track him down in the future.

But no... She couldn't possibly. They were strangers, which was how it should be. She was a fire witch, hunted by all. And he was... What *was* he?

Whatever he was, he was likely someone she wouldn't want to associate with. Not if he wasn't mortal and associated with other gods.

He looked at her, his eyes brighter than before, highlighting the silver within them. For the first time, Marina noticed he had identical silver streaks in his hair as well, though he didn't look nearly old enough for his hair to start graying.

No, this wasn't gray hair. It was some other mark. A mark of magic.

With a smirk, he adjusted her skirts around her, replacing her bodice so it covered her breasts. Though her flesh had been cold before, the feel of fabric against it instead of his hands was loathsome. She almost wanted to rip her dress off entirely, knowing nothing would ever touch her the same way again.

She wished she had had more of him. More of his skin, of his body entangled with hers. To take her against a wall like this was perfect for feral pleasure, but now that it was over, she found herself wishing she'd taken her time with him, savoring the muscles and planes of his body.

And now it was too late.

"My beautiful blue jay," the man murmured, running his hand along her cheek.

Marina wanted to say something clever, something witty that would linger with him the way he lingered with her. But words escaped her as he lowered his hand and melted into the shadows. She almost cried out when he vanished entirely, knowing it was too late.

Knowing she would never see him again.

Marina jerked awake, squinting against the intense bright light of the sun. She must have fallen asleep in the temple. Well, that was no surprise. Her devious fox had quite thoroughly exhausted her.

But as her foggy mind adjusted, and her eyes took in the scene before her, she realized it was *not* the sun shining on her. It was magic.

With a jolt, she sat up, her dress rumpled and her mask askew on her face. A woman stood before her with thick, springy curls and blazing silver eyes, her skin a warm copper. She wore a loose white dress and a tiara of aquamarine gemstones on her head, similar to the one Remy had worn the night before. Gold light flowed from her fingertips, and her hair lifted around her as if she were submerged in water.

Marina's breath caught in her throat, her eyes wide and her throat dry as she took in the glowing figure before her. She wasn't sure what was happening, but she knew one thing: this woman was a goddess.

Marina immediately bowed herself before the figure, pressing her face toward the ground, arms shaking.

"You dare insult me with such false respect?" the goddess cried, her voice resonating like the sound of a thousand voices. "When you have already defiled my sacred temple?"

Marina's body iced over with the chill of her realization. This was Tethys, Goddess of the river. The goddess Marina's coven worshiped fervently.

"Blessed be the Goddess," Marina whispered, shutting her eyes, willing this all to go away, to vanish like some horrible nightmare. She was dreaming, surely. That must be it. "Have mercy on my soul. Blessed be the Goddess."

"Spare me," Tethys shrieked, and something akin to lightning split through the temple with an almighty *crack.*

Marina flinched, expecting the ceiling to cave in and crush her, for this goddess to kill her on the spot. "I beg your forgiveness, Queen of the Rivers. I—I was careless and foolish. My actions were unwise and thoughtless."

"You truly have no idea just what you've done, have you?" Tethys's voice grew deadly quiet, and Marina almost preferred her shouting. This softer tone was lethal.

Hesitantly, Marina peered up at the goddess, who watched her with narrowed eyes, her upper lip curling in disgust.

"*Fire witch,*" Tethys spat. "You sully my name with your presence here. Not only that, but you defile my sacred house with a death god!"

Death god. Marina was shaking her head. "No. *No!* He—I did not—"

"Yes, it was a death god you tumbled with, you filthy wretch. Have you no restraint? No self-control? Your careless behavior threatened the sacred laws of Elysium *and* the Underworld. You could have caused unholy destruction between our realms, igniting a war of gods."

The masked man had been a *death god*? Marina couldn't think past the raging turmoil of her confusion. It was impossible. There was no way...

But she had heard stories of gods roaming the Realm of Gaia, if only for a brief period of time. *I can only remain here for a short time before I am... summoned back home,* he'd said.

Bile crept up her throat, but she forced it down and

whispered, "I did not know. He was only one man. He was alone! I—I thought it would mean nothing."

"He is a son of Aidoneus, creator of the Underworld," Tethys said coldly. "Should Aidoneus seek retribution, he would be well within his right to wage war against me and all the witches who follow me. Because *you* chose my holy sanctuary for your filthy deeds."

Marina's head was spinning. All she could do was shake her head, too numb to speak. *What would Remy say?* Her mother would be so disappointed...

But that didn't matter now. Surely, this goddess was here to kill her. Marina would never see Remy again. She shut her eyes, waiting for the blow to come, for Tethys to inflict punishment on her.

"Death would be too swift for you, foul witch," Tethys hissed as if reading her mind. "No. You should suffer. I curse you, Marina the fire witch, to roam this land for all eternity, to never know love or companionship, to suffer a life of solitude and loneliness. May your days be lengthened to show you just how pitiful your existence truly is. May all who draw close to you, who dare to show love for you, be smitten by my curse."

Another strike of lightning, another crack in the air. A blast of searing white light burned against Marina's eyes, and she flinched away from it, cowering from the goddess's power.

When the light faded, Tethys had vanished, leaving Marina shaking and alone in the temple. Her skin was cold and clammy, her face covered in sweat. She rose on trembling legs, ripping the mask from her face and stumbling out of the temple.

Dawn had just broken, and the forest was silent around her. This wasn't unusual, since the morning after Litha was often quiet with the aftermath of too much revelry and alcohol.

But this was different. A chill of foreboding swept over Marina, raising bumps along her flesh and stoking the fire magic roiling within her. The goddess's words rang in her mind: *May all who draw close to you, who dare to show love for you, be smitten by my curse.*

She thought of only one thing: Remy.

Her steps hastened as she practically sprinted down the hill and toward the forest path. She knew this trail well; she could practically walk it blindfolded. Her breaths grew sharp and heavy with each step. *Please, please, please.*

The entire forest screamed its silence at her. Even the animals and insects were hushed, leaving a gaping emptiness that pressed in on her as she ran. The only sounds were her own panting and the thumping of her feet along the moist leaves and dirt.

Marina reached the bridge that crested the Snake

River and froze. The usual roaring rush of water was absent, and now she saw why.

The river had been turned to stone.

What had once been a constant flow of motion, with shades of turquoise and aquamarine glistening in the sunlight, was now a pale, cold gray. No movement. No sparkling waters. The twisting current and bubbles had been frozen like moments in time, the curves and ripples forever preserved in a sculpture that would never move again.

Tears pricked Marina's eyes as she gazed at the depths that had once been so soothing. Now, the river was dead.

Panic clenched her chest, and she hurried across the bridge and toward her home. The path wound downhill, and she passed several small dwellings where her neighbors lived. Not a soul was in sight. Even the morning after Litha, there were a few witches roaming about. But not now.

Marina raced toward Remy's small cottage, a stitch forming in her side and sweat pouring down her body. When she burst inside, she shrieked, "Mama? *Mama!*"

No answer.

Marina checked the kitchen and dining area. Nothing. The house was silent as the grave.

Perhaps she is with Giselle, Marina told herself. *Perhaps she has already risen and started her day.*

But the sense of foreboding clawed at her chest like a beast. Tears were now streaming down her face. She ran down the hall and into Remy's bedroom, then stopped short.

There she was, the woman who had raised and loved Marina more than anyone, lying motionless on the bed, her body completely turned to stone. Her eyes were closed with sleep, her body on its side, legs curled up as she so often slept, her hair a mane fanned out behind her.

She was a statue. Her rich brown hair was now pale gray; her face, which had once been tan and healthy, now nothing more than coarse rock.

Marina sank to her knees, sobs wracking through her. "Mama," she wailed, tilting her face to the floor as she wept openly. "Mama, wake up, *please!*"

There was no answer.

Broken and desperate, Marina crawled toward the edge of the bed, stretching her hand out to clasp Remy's. It was cold and rough against her skin, nothing like the smooth and soothing touch she was accustomed to.

"Please, Mama," she moaned. "Please wake up."

She knelt there for hours, sobbing while she held her mother's hand and willed her to come back, to open her eyes, to wake from Tethys's curse.

But she didn't.

And when Marina's tears dried up, her body aching

from crouching by the bed for so long, her eyes swollen and her heart shattered, she finally unleashed herself, unable to hold back any more.

Fire exploded from within her, consuming everything; the floorboards, the walls, the ceiling, the furniture... Everything went up in flames. Marina screamed as the inferno tore through her, brutal and merciless. And as her fire magic devoured everything in sight, she felt her body shifting, elongating. A low hiss built up in her throat as her skin changed. Sharp fangs extended in her mouth. Her arms disappeared into her torso as her skin stretched and stretched and stretched. Distantly, she knew she should feel alarmed or scared of this transformation, but all she felt was rage and agony fueling her, driving her forward.

Power emanated from her as she morphed into a giant snake, unleashing an almighty screech of devastation.

And still, Marina burned.

CHAPTER TWO
FIFTY YEARS LATER

MARINA ADJUSTED HER SCARF TO BETTER conceal her face as the brisk desert wind whipped at her, stinging her eyes with sand particles. Her skin was already caked with grains of it, her lips dry and cracked, her throat burning. It would be so much easier if she shifted to her snake form and traveled that way, but then she would be unable to carry her items with her. Her blades were snug inside her belt, a heavy comfort with each step she took.

As a fire witch, she was often hunted and despised. Over the years, she had learned to defend herself with a blade. It became a necessity.

Not that it mattered. Once, she'd been skewered by the sword of a soldier, impaled right through the chest. It hadn't killed her. Tethys's curse had kept her alive.

But the recovery had been the most brutal pain she had ever endured. If she could avoid that pain again, she would.

No, it was easier to disarm her opponent with a few swift strikes and flee, unscathed, than to allow herself to become mortally wounded and have to wait for her body to heal.

Because while Tethys had granted her immortality, she had not given her the indestructible body of a goddess. Marina was still human and suffered all human frailties.

Bitterness and rage burned within her, igniting her fire magic, but she suppressed it for now. The idea of revenge burned bright in her mind, reminding her of why she was here.

She would find a way to destroy Tethys. She had all eternity to do it.

Marina glanced down at the worn scrap of parchment she clutched in her hands, detailing everything she knew about the coven that dwelt here in the Rhea Desert.

It wasn't much.

Marina had spent years searching archives and texts, traveling from coven to coven for information about Tethys. Some water covens had been welcoming, believing her lie that she was a traveling earth witch in search of refuge for the night. Others had been hostile, requiring Marina to unsheathe her blades to defend herself.

But one day, she stumbled upon an ancient folktale of Neptune and Hestia and their brutal feud. Neptune and Tethys were allies, both deities of water. But Hestia, the fire goddess, was despised by them both. For centuries, the two sides had been at war with one another... which would explain why Tethys had hated Marina so much—enough to curse her for one passionate night.

A night with a death god.

But Marina wouldn't allow herself to dwell on him. Whoever he was, he had vanished and never returned. He had left Marina to suffer her fate—to live a life of solitude for all eternity, cursed to watch everyone she cared about turn to stone.

One day she would get her revenge on him, too. But first... Tethys.

Water witches knew nothing of Hestia, unfortunately. But one tale told of an ancient tribe of fire witches, blessed by Hestia, who lived in a hidden colony in the desert, impossible to find.

If anyone could locate them, it was Marina. Even if her body suffered from thirst or starvation, she would only recover and continue her pursuit. She would spend years in these sands if that was what it took.

Marina stared hard at the scrap of parchment. *Only*

those with fire magic can locate the entrance. For decades, she had suppressed her magic, only unleashing it when she had access to an empty, unoccupied, wide open space. She knew firsthand what happened when she didn't loose her fire every now and then.

Still. After all these years, she had never trusted herself to use it regularly. Not only did it paint a target on her back, but her fire magic had caused so much grief and destruction already.

And yet, here she was, at long last, seeking out her own people.

Discomfort wriggled through her at the thought. She had spent so much of her life learning to fear and despise her magic. After losing her entire coven and enduring a curse—all because of the magic she wielded —it was hard for her to simply accept it.

The more she researched, the more she understood that Tethys had cursed her, not for *defiling her temple,* as she claimed, nor for dallying with a death god. No, Tethys had acted out of an ancient vendetta against Hestia and all fire witches.

So, if anyone knew how to fight back, it would be Hestia herself.

Marina crested down a steep hill, sand sliding along her sandals as she struggled to keep her balance. She squinted against the desert wind, trying to make out shapes before her, but all she saw was a swirling vortex. The beginnings of a sandstorm.

"Shit," Marina muttered, tightening her scarf around her face. She wasn't afraid of the sandstorm, but she didn't particularly like the idea of being swept up in it, turned around, and possibly dumped out farther away from her destination than she intended. The fire within her raged, eager to be unleashed.

Gritting her teeth, Marina scurried forward, making out a vague shape in the distance: a formation of rocks and boulders.

Perfect.

Marina's stride lengthened as she tried to outrun the storm, her pack slinging against her hip and jingling with each step. The wind picked up, roaring against her ears, the sand in the air making it almost impossible to see. Her breathing was labored, each inhale bringing dust particles along with it. Her throat felt like coarse pebbles. Her skin burned.

At long last, she reached the first boulder and threw herself over it, crouching down low to use the rocks as cover. She buried her face between her legs, tying her pack around the boulder twice to keep it in place.

"That won't help!" shouted a voice.

Marina's head snapped up as she made out a figure standing above her. She had thick, black hair and brown skin, but her *eyes...* They shone bright amber. Just like Marina's did when her fire magic was unleashed.

Fire witch.

No longer concerned with the sandstorm, Marina rose to her feet. She stood taller than the woman, but not by much.

"Who are you?" the witch asked. "Why are you here?"

The wind billowed around them. Marina winced as the sand struck her skin with vicious intensity. "I'm seeking refuge." She scanned the rocks, wondering where the woman had come from. "Is your home nearby?"

The woman cocked her head at Marina, assessing her. "I sense our magic within you. But it's... tainted. I'll ask again—who are you?"

"My name is Marina. I've been on the run for a very long time. I'm only here to seek answers about my magic."

The woman's eyes narrowed slightly. After a moment, she nodded. "Follow me."

The sandstorm roared, and Marina was quick to hurry after the witch as she descended deeper into the rocks. Marina's feet slid against the sandy boulders and pebbles, and she grabbed onto the rocks for purchase. They followed a narrow path Marina hadn't noticed before, one that wound between the boulders and descended far below them. The lower they went, the more the sounds of the storm receded, until Marina found herself at the mouth of a cave buried beneath the rocks. Invisible from the outside.

"Incredible," Marina murmured, eyes wide with awe.

The woman abruptly turned to face her. Without warning, she summoned a ball of flame and pressed it into Marina's palm. Marina shrieked, trying to jerk her hand away, but the woman held fast. The fire didn't burn Marina, but the shock of it sent a bolt of awareness coursing through her, igniting her fire magic. A blast of power rocketed through her, and she arched backward with a feral cry, feeling the presence of her serpent on the verge of breaking free.

Just as suddenly, the woman withdrew, dousing the flames. Marina gasped as the magic left her, her snake receding and her body going stiff. Panting, she demanded, "What the hell was that?"

The woman offered a wry smile. "I had to be certain. We don't let just anyone take shelter here."

Marina swallowed hard, her throat still dry as a bone, and nodded.

"I'm Farah," the woman said, inclining her head. "Coven leader. Welcome to the Rhea Coven."

CHAPTER THREE

Farah guided Marina down a dark, winding path that led deeper into the caves. The darkness swallowed Marina completely, and she had to brace her hands against the rocky walls to keep herself from tripping. Farah was unperturbed—she likely knew this path by heart, having traveled it so often. Every time Marina stumbled, Farah paused and waited patiently for her to catch up.

After what felt like hours, the tunnel opened up to a vast cavern lit by torches. Small benches surrounded a fire pit, achingly reminding Marina of the sacred stone circle from her river coven. Witches sat on the benches, chatting with one another. They fell silent as Farah and Marina entered the space. Each woman stood, bowing her head in reverence to the coven leader.

Every single witch had amber-colored eyes, just like Farah. But other than that, they couldn't have been more different. Most of the witches had dark brown or black hair, but others had red or blond hair. Some were darker-skinned, like Farah. Others had a more olive skin tone, some a deeper brown, almost black. Few were as pale as Marina, which made her wonder if something was truly wrong with her and her magic. Had she suppressed it for so long that her body would never be the same?

"This is Marina." Farah gestured behind her. "She is seeking temporary refuge among us."

Marina didn't miss how Farah emphasized *temporary*. But that was fine with her. The longer she stayed, the more at risk this coven would be. She had already witnessed firsthand what would happen to someone who dared to care for her. Just as Tethys foretold, they turned to stone. Every time. Even when Marina tried her hardest not to be likable.

"What's wrong with her?" asked a witch with curly auburn hair.

Marina stiffened at her bluntness, her anger rising, but Farah answered before she could.

"Her magic has been suppressed. We will help her unlock it. But for now, she needs a place to rest. Tilly, will you prepare a room for her?"

A woman with short cropped blond hair and tan skin

stood and strode to the edge of the cave, disappearing down one of the winding tunnels.

The remaining witches stared openly at Marina, apparently not concerned with rudeness or propriety. Marina fidgeted under their gazes, her skin feeling itchy. She wanted to leave this place, to avoid *unlocking her magic*, as Farah put it. That wasn't her intent at all. She needed to access the archives here, uncover answers about Hestia, and leave as soon as possible. Fire witches were already dying around the realm. The last thing Marina wanted to do was add to that number.

She turned to Farah to ask if there was a library somewhere within these caves, but the words died in her throat as the coven leader's eyes closed, her entire form trembling. Fire coated her hands and arms, and her body began to elongate and shift.

Stunned, Marina staggered back a step, watching as Farah shed her clothes and hair, her body growing scales and stretching long until she resembled a serpent—a cobra, in particular, but different from Marina's white form. This snake was tawny, with umber-colored spots along its scales.

Marina swallowed hard. She couldn't believe her eyes. *Another* snake shifter? She gazed around the room at the other witches, but they all looked on calmly. Then, another witch began to shift, her body trembling and quivering just as Farah's had. After a moment, she transformed into another cobra, this one much lighter in color.

Marina couldn't breathe. She clutched at her chest, trying to inhale, to steady her pulse. How was this possible?

"You thought you were the only one?"

Marina blinked and found the auburn-haired witch standing next to her with a sly smile on her face.

"The only what?" Marina asked.

"Snake shifter." The witch gestured to Marina's figure. "Though I've never seen one with your coloring before. That's rare."

"Coloring?" Marina's mind couldn't keep up. She was still baffled by the presence of other snake shifters. All this time, she'd thought her snake form had been part of Tethys's curse.

"Our skin tone matches the coloring of our snake's scales," the woman explained. "All of us here are cobras, but I've never seen a white one before." She tilted her head, assessing Marina with cold calculation. "What are you?"

"I don't know." Marina's voice was hollow, but she spoke the truth. "I was abandoned as a child. Raised by water witches."

The woman snorted. "Goddess. That must have been terrible."

A lump formed in Marina's throat, and she shook her

head. "They were kind to take me in. They didn't understand my magic. No one did. Not even me."

The woman's expression softened. "I'm sorry you didn't have a proper mentor to train you. But you're here now, and we'll do what we can."

Marina stiffened at the kindness of the woman's words, the echoes of her curse ringing in her ears. "It isn't safe for you—for anyone—to get too close to me."

The witch's amber eyes flashed. "I can tell your magic is tainted by something else. Some other power. You reek of it, Marina. Whatever secrets you hold, I want no part of them, so don't you worry. I'll keep my distance." She lifted her chin. "My name is Wren."

"Wren like the bird?"

Wren offered a wolfish smile. "I was named after my first kill."

"Oh." Marina's stomach turned with discomfort.

Wren laughed. "You'll get used to it. Goddess, being around water witches has turned you soft."

Shame and grief swelled in Marina's chest at the reminder of the coven, the home, the family she'd lost. She looked away, her gaze sweeping around the room. Two more witches had shifted into snakes, the large serpents slithering along the rocky floors. Marina, who had never been around so many snakes in her life, should have been frightened by this. How many times had Remy warned her about poisonous vipers in the woods?

But, strangely, she felt nothing but a silent surety, a calmness down to her bones. Even her fire magic had been quelled by the presence of these kindred spirits.

"It's almost hunting time," Wren said. "Once the storm settles, there's prey ripe for the picking." She licked her lips, revealing two sharpened fangs.

Marina shuddered, and Wren laughed again. Marina got the feeling this witch enjoyed making her feel uncomfortable.

The ground shook, and dust sprinkled from the ceiling. The walls quivered, and Marina's hands flew out as she almost toppled to the ground. Breathless, she asked, "Is that the storm?"

"No." Wren's expression had grown solemn as she stared up at the rocky ceiling.

A flash of white light flared in the center of the room, and in an instant, Farah was back in her witch form, fully clothed and eyes blazing with determination. The walls shook again, and a feral roar echoed from one of the tunnels.

"Wren," Farah commanded. "With me."

Wren nodded, striding to stand next to Farah. Together, they raced to the other end of the cavern, disappearing into the narrow tunnel where the shout had come from. Marina stood, stiff as a board, itching to join them just to see what the commotion was. But she knew she would get lost in seconds, and even if she *could* keep up, what good would she be? Her magic was useless.

Several other snakes had shifted back to their human forms, bustling about gathering items in their arms. As Marina watched them, she realized they were throwing together ingredients into a large cauldron. One of them hoisted the cauldron and lowered it into the fire pit.

They were creating a spell.

This Marina could help with. She surged forward, determination burning in her blood. She recognized lavender and eucalyptus leaves being dumped into the cauldron. A binding spell, perhaps. Her gaze roved over the room until she saw a row of shelves built into the opposite wall. She rushed over to it, scanning the contents until she found what she was looking for: wormwood. She snatched the jar and brought it over to the cauldron.

A witch with black dreadlocks stood in her path, her expression hard. "What are you doing?"

"Wormwood." Marina lifted the jar. "It subdues foreign magic. If there's an intruder here, we don't know what kind of magic we're dealing with."

The witch scowled, then glanced at the other women.

"She's right," muttered a blond witch. "I was just

going after that ingredient myself." She nodded her approval. "Well done."

The black-haired witch grumbled something unintelligible before stepping back to allow Marina access to the cauldron. After dumping the wormwood inside, several witches began chanting in a language Marina didn't understand. She withdrew a few steps, not wanting to interfere with the magic churning in the air, but the blond witch gestured her forward, extending her hands.

Alarmed, Marina approached slowly, swallowing down the lump of emotion in her throat. She took the witch's hand, inserting herself into the sacred circle. The last time she had participated in one of these had been the night of Litha. The night her curse had been thrust upon her and her entire coven had been slaughtered by Tethys's fury.

Marina's chest ached, tightening and coiling like a serpent. Tears stung her eyes, and she impatiently blinked them away.

Never again, she vowed. *I will not let that happen again.*

She would leave here as soon as she possibly could. Already, it seemed a few witches were a bit too welcoming of her. How long before Tethys's fury struck them, too?

Marina wouldn't wait around to find out. She shut her eyes, focusing on the words of the enchantment instead. After a moment, she placed the language: Latin. The river coven hadn't used much Latin in their spells, unfortunately, but after a few repetitions, Marina was able to piece out some syllables and utter the phrases along with the other witches. The contents of the cauldron bubbled and churned, and an eerie amber smoke wafted from within—the exact same color as the witches' eyes.

Fire magic. *Snake* magic.

More shouts echoed from the tunnels, and Marina stiffened. The blond witch squeezed her hand in reassurance. Then, a shrill, animalistic screech pierced the air, making the ground tremble.

The sound was inhuman. It had to be some kind of powerful monster.

Another screech filled the cavern, this one coming from one of the other tunnels. The witches around Marina jumped in alarm, their eyes darting from one tunnel to the next.

There was more than one. Whatever creature was here, it hadn't come alone.

The witches' chanting grew in volume, as if they could chase away the danger with the power of their voices. Dread crept down Marina's spine as the walls trembled again.

"What if the cave collapses?" Marina asked over the sound of the chanting. "Shouldn't we flee?"

The blond witch shook her head, leaning in to whisper in Marina's ear. "Farah has it warded. It can't collapse unless someone unravels her spells."

This wasn't very reassuring. What if the intruders *were* magical? What if they could take down this cave, despite Farah's wards?

The shrieking continued, and another sound followed after. Some distant thumping, like footsteps, only heavier and faster. Movement appeared at the mouth of the opposite tunnel. Instinct had Marina unsheathing her blades, breaking free of the witches' circle and darting forward to meet her opponent.

Another loud screech, but the creature was close enough for Marina to distinguish the sound. It wasn't a screech, but a loud, sharp, *whinny.* And the thumping was more of a clopping. Like hoofbeats.

Marina's skin chilled as a massive horse burst through the tunnel, the archway crumbling and raining dust and rocks on its head. But it was unperturbed... because the horse itself was made completely of sand.

Marina's heart lurched in her throat. She had never seen a creature like this before. She had seen horses, yes, but this one stood twice as tall as her, and its entire body rippled like the waves of the sea. Sand and dust trickled along its body, shifting and moving as if it were part of the sandstorm.

The sandstorm. Had this creature come from the

storm outside? Was there some kind of otherworldly magic at play here?

A scream echoed in the other tunnel, this one human. Alarm pulsed through Marina as she thought of Wren and Farah. How could they fight a creature like this—a creature whose body could not be pierced? Marina's hands were slick with sweat as she clutched her blades, knowing they would do no good. Those rocks had passed right through the horse's body.

"*Protego!*" shouted a voice.

Marina turned and found the blond witch had also broken from the circle and raised her palm. Bright red magic flared to life, bursting in the air and surrounding the cavern. The air shimmered, and a faint transparent dome encircled the crowd of witches, including Marina.

The horse reared its head and bounded forward, slamming directly into the barrier. The ground shook, and the barrier flickered, but it held fast. It would protect them, but not for long.

Another whinny echoed in the tunnels as a second sand horse appeared, careening toward Marina. She flinched, even knowing the barrier was in place. As it collided with the magic, the ground shook again, more violently this time. Marina stumbled, falling to her knees from the impact.

"What are they?" Marina cried, glancing over her shoulder.

The blond witch stared, horrified, as the creatures alternated blows against her magic. "I don't know. But their magic is ancient. Stronger than mine." She turned to the witches still standing in a circle. "Sisters! Together!" She inserted herself back into the circle and clasped hands. The chanting continued, and red magic flowed from the cauldron, spiraling in the air.

Marina watched them, torn between joining their circle and trying to fight off the beasts herself. Gritting her teeth, she sheathed her daggers and spread her hands, calling upon the fire still churning just under her skin. She kept it suppressed so often that when she *did* conjure it, it came to life almost effortlessly.

Flames appeared along her fingertips. She pushed, drawing out more of her power until her arms were coated in fire. She threw her head back and screamed, unleashing it all. With her scream, flames burned her throat, searing her insides, scorching her body. She let it consume her completely. Soon, all she saw was the amber inferno of her magic. She didn't hear the witches' chanting or the horses' whinnies. She *became* the fire.

Her magic coaxed her onward, and she gave it complete control. The power within her pulled, tugging her toward the threat. Her fire melted right through the barrier until she stood before the closest horse. She hissed, baring her teeth as her fangs emerged. White scales formed along her skin, and her body elongated, her head rising until she stood as tall as the horse itself.

Then, she struck.

At first, she only tasted sand and dirt, the particles trickling off the horses' body like nothing more than water droplets. But with her next strike, she infused it with her own fire, burying her fangs deep into the horse's neck.

The horse screamed, rearing back in surprise as Marina's fangs met something solid. Something fleshy.

Underneath the hide of indestructible sand was a body of flesh and bone. It *could* be killed.

Encouraged by this, Marina struck again and again, her fangs sinking deeper with each assault. Her relentless advances had the horse backing away from her, its back pressing into the rocky wall behind it.

Magic surged behind her, and the sounds of hissing filled the air. The other witches were shifting, too, perhaps spurred on by Marina's success. Cobras wriggled along the dusty ground, and pulses of red magic continued spiraling in the air, spreading the magic from their spell. One snake raised itself up like Marina and began to strike at the second horse. When the horse retaliated, rearing on its hind legs, coils of red magic floated to the witch's defense, surrounding her and protecting her from its hooves.

Several other snakes joined Marina, and together,

they surrounded the sand horse. Marina continued to cut with her fangs while another snake slithered over the horse's body, winding and coiling, tightening until the horse shrieked in agony.

The ceiling quivered, and boulders rained from above. Marina slithered out of the way, narrowly avoiding getting crushed. Another scream filled the air, this one closer than before.

Then, from behind the second horse appeared a pair of figures. Wren and Farah. Farah was holding up an unconscious Wren, whose head was covered in blood. They stumbled forward, narrowly avoiding getting stomped on by the sand horse. Just as they collapsed in the middle of the cavern, another horse appeared at the mouth of the tunnel. More whinnies echoed from within the caves.

How many more were there? Would they just keep coming until the witches had all been killed?

Marina's body shuddered as she tried to rein in her serpent form, but it resisted. It wanted to stay free, to continue with the battle. She wrenched her fire magic back, receding far, far within herself, commanding the snake to shift.

I am in control, she thought.

Are you? answered a voice. *Or do I merely allow you to believe that?*

Icy coldness filled Marina's body at the sound of that

voice. The sound of her serpent. Panic rose up inside her. Was she enslaved to the snake? To her magic?

But just as her panic mounted, her form began to change as she shed her skin, her human form taking the place of her white serpent. She glanced down to find herself completely naked. Somewhere behind her were her clothes and weapons, but she didn't have time to grab them. Ignoring her exposed body, she raced over to Farah and helped her ease Wren onto a bench.

Farah, to her credit, didn't blink at Marina's nudity. "There are two more in the tunnels," she said breathlessly. "They won't stop."

"What are they?" Marina asked, checking Wren's body for a pulse. There it was; steady, but weak.

"Kelpies," Farah said. "Mutated variations of Neptune's hippocampi. The average hippocampus can only travel through bodies of water, but kelpies? They can shift and morph, just like us, to adapt to different landforms." She shook her head, her nostrils flaring. "They are born of an ancient magic. A magic I thought was gone forever."

"How are they here?" Marina asked, glancing at the horses, who were still being viciously attacked by the snakes. But as another horse appeared in the mouth of the tunnel, Marina knew they were about to be severely outnumbered.

"I don't know. When they roamed the realm before,

it was thousands of years ago. Hestia and the water gods were at war. Tethys used a forbidden magic to craft a dark, sentient being that could hunt Hestia's fire shifters. They were banished long ago by Hestia herself."

Hestia. Marina's skin prickled with awareness, her heart racing. This was it. These were the answers she'd been searching for. But right now, while these witches were in grave peril, it was hard for her to process it fully. "If Hestia banished them before, how do we stop them *now?*"

Farah's eyes flashed. "We can't. We don't have enough power. There's a reason we live in the desert—it makes it more difficult for the water goddess to track us down. But with kelpies on the loose? It's only a matter of time before they find us and kill us all."

"But they *can* be killed," Marina insisted, gesturing to the horse she'd been attacking. It had slumped to the ground, practically motionless as the other snakes finished it off.

"Temporarily," Farah said. "The dark magic will reawaken them in time. Only the power of a goddess can destroy them for good. Even if we weren't outnumbered, by the time we take out all these kelpies, the first ones will be reawakening. We *must* flee."

Marina nodded, her body stiffening as a hissing cry filled the air. One of the snakes collapsed, blood gushing from a wound along its scales.

Marina didn't remember rising to her feet. All she knew was the bloodlust burning within her, her fire magic still raging at being caged once more. She darted forward, swiping one of the blades from her pile of clothes as she ran. Summoning her fire magic, she brought the flames to life in her palms, allowing it to coat her blade in an amber glow. She roared with fury, racing toward the horse that had wounded one of the witches. Marina raised her arms and buried the blade straight into the kelpie's throat. The creature reared its head, trying to jerk away, but Marina buried her blade deeper and deeper, coaxing more of her flames into it. She sliced down, down, down, cutting all the way through, feeling the resistance of muscle and bone from within.

In an explosion of sand and dust, the horse's head came clean off its body, disintegrating into nothingness. The sand burst in the air, stinging Marina's eyes.

Triumph burned in her chest at the creature's demise, but it was short-lived. Two more kelpies appeared and charged at her.

"Shit," Marina whispered. She turned and fled, aiming for her clothing and her second dagger.

Before she could reach it, a rush of black smoke filled the cavern, rising up and twining with the red magic of the witches. Marina stilled, staring at the darkness as it seeped into the cave, swarming around the kelpies. The smoke was so thick that Marina couldn't see through it, but she could hear the screeching of the kelpies... and the desperate hissing of the snakes.

What was happening? Was this from the kelpies or something else?

"Farah!" Marina shouted, stumbling forward, trying to reach someone, to *help*—

A sudden silence rang against her ears, eerily reminding her of that cold emptiness just before she had discovered her entire coven had been killed. Dread numbed her body, the horrors of that morning replaying in her mind again and again.

No, no, no...

"Marina! Are you all right?" Farah called.

Marina's breath returned to her in a rush, her head spinning. She choked out, "Yes!"

Gradually, the black smoke dispersed. Marina waved a hand in front of her face to help clear it, squinting through the haze. The red magic had vanished... and so had the kelpies.

Panting, Marina surged forward, scanning the area to see what had happened. A few witches remained, now in human form... but there weren't nearly as many as there had been before. The snakes that were attacking the kelpies had all vanished, too.

Farah was hurrying toward her, eyes wide with panic. "What happened? What did you do?"

"That—That wasn't me," Marina said, her voice trembling.

"It was me."

Farah and Marina turned toward the voice, which was deep and distinctly male. A tall figure stood in the middle of the cavern, face shining with sweat and blazing with intensity.

Marina's heart lurched, her insides freezing over with recognition. The man had inky black hair streaked with silver, and identical silver eyes that haunted Marina every night, reminding her of what she'd lost.

It was *him*. The masked man. The fox.

The death god.

CHAPTER FOUR

One second, Marina was staring, horrified, at the death god who had ruined her life.

The next, she was flying across the cavern with inhuman speed, pressing her blade to the god's neck and baring her teeth.

"Bastard," she growled, reveling in the way his eyes widened and his throat bobbed. "How dare you show your face here?"

"Marina," Farah warned.

"I've met this god," Marina said without taking her eyes off him. "He's dangerous and deceitful. You would do well to end him right now, before he has a chance to destroy your life the way he destroyed mine. I wouldn't be surprised if *he* brought the kelpies here."

"I didn't," the god said. Emotion flared in his silvery

eyes, thick and potent. "Jay... I—I never meant for any of it to happen. I didn't *know*."

"Bullshit," Marina snapped, pressing her blade hard enough to draw a drop of silver blood.

"Marina!" Farah chided, her voice ringing out, echoing in the vast cavern. The authority in her tone made Marina stiffen with realization. Every pair of eyes was on her, narrowed with suspicion and distrust.

She had just admitted to knowing a death god. A god who clearly didn't care one whit for mortal witches and who likely had brought these dark creatures on the coven's doorstep.

Slowly, Marina withdrew her hand, but she kept her dagger poised. The god still watched her with wide eyes, his gaze flicking down her body and his face reddening as he undoubtedly realized she wore no clothes.

"Why are you here?" she demanded. "What did you do to the kelpies and the witches?"

"Witches?" His face paled. "My magic only targeted creatures born of magic."

Farah swore. "You *fool*! This entire coven is made up of magical creatures! We are snake shifters, descended from the Gorgons themselves."

The god's face now turned an ashy gray, his eyes wide and horrified.

"Where did you send them?" Farah demanded, striding closer. "Tell me!"

"I sent them to the origin of all death magic. But—"

Farah unleashed a feral shout of rage, her teeth bared and her amber eyes flaring with the rise of her magic. She lunged for the god, and Marina was about to join her, when he raised his hands and shouted, "They are still in this realm! I swear it!"

Farah faltered. "Explain."

"Pandora's box has been opened."

A hushed silence fell in the cavern, and Marina swore an eerie ripple of otherworldly power brushed over them like a hissing wind. Bumps rose along her arms and neck, and she suppressed a shudder.

"The dark forces within the box destroyed the Underworld," the god went on. "Those creatures were created by Tethys, but she used death magic to bring them to being. They were born of death magic, the same magic I possess. They do not *have* a home to return to. I don't know for sure where they were sent... perhaps to a portal that leads to the Underworld, like the one that brought me here."

"Brought you here?" Marina repeated.

He gestured behind him toward the tunnels. "The portal. That's how I came here. Listen, I don't have time—"

But Marina whirled to Farah. "You have a *portal* here? One that leads to the realm of the gods?"

"We were blessed by the magic of Hestia herself," Farah said, lifting her chin. "Of course we have a portal."

Marina shook her head in disbelief. Somewhere within these tunnels was a direct path to the gods themselves. If Marina used it, could she reach Tethys and kill her? Her deepest desire was only steps away…

"Perhaps the kelpies and the witches are waiting for us by that portal now," speculated a blond witch.

But the god shook his head. "I can sense the magic of the kelpies. They aren't anywhere within these caves."

"And even if they were," Farah added, "the portal is useless now. It takes a powerful arsenal of magic to fuel it, and it is likely drained from *this one's* arrival." She waved a hand toward the god with a snarl. "The kelpies have no reason to be drawn to our portal when it is depleted of energy." She drew closer to the god, her eyes glinting with lethal intensity. "Bring my witches back," she commanded him. "*Now.*"

"I cannot. My magic is—" The god broke off with a strangled gasp, his face turning white and his eyes rolling back.

Startled, Marina took a step away from him, eyes wide as she watched him fall to his knees. "What's wrong with him?"

Just as suddenly, the god sucked in a breath, his eyes returning to their normal silver as he staggered to his feet, his body unsteady.

"Jay," he gasped, his eyes drilling into hers, pleading. "*Marina.*"

Goddess, the sound of her name on those lips... Marina was torn between slapping him in the face and begging him to say her name once more, just so she could savor it.

"The day you were cursed, so was I," he said. "I was cursed, bound to the Underworld, unable to travel between realms. I tried to return to you. To *help* you."

Marina scoffed. Even if he *had* returned, what could he have done? Tethys's curse had already bound Marina's fate. Nothing could have changed that, especially not death magic.

Murmurs rippled among the other witches, and Marina shifted her weight from one foot to the other.

"Cursed?" Farah repeated, her amber eyes fixed on Marina. "You never mentioned a curse, Marina."

"*You* never mentioned having a portal," Marina snapped. "My curse will not affect you. Not if I take my leave soon. I only need some information, and then I'll be on my way."

"What information?" Farah asked, but the death god interrupted her.

"You aren't hearing me," he said, his voice sharpening. "I'm here because the Underworld has been destroyed by Pandora's magic. *More* creatures like those kelpies will be here soon. I don't have long before I—"

He went rigid again, his spine straightening, the muscles in his arms and throat working desperately as if he couldn't breathe. His back arched, and a pained groan escaped his lips.

Marina's body was frozen, her mind torn between terror and panic at the sight of him like this. She couldn't help the swell of emotion burning within her. Even knowing he was despicable and responsible for her curse, she felt a strange sense of concern for him. She didn't like to see him in pain. Despite how much he deserved it.

When the god opened his eyes, they were all black.

Marina drew in a gasp. "He *is* cursed."

Black smoke began to pour from the god's mouth, filling the air. A foul stench followed—the smell of death magic.

Marina raced forward, grabbing the god by the shoulders and shaking him vigorously. "Fox! *Fox!* Stop this, now! You'll kill us!"

The instant her skin touched his, something jolted through her, scorching her bones and igniting her fire. She sucked in a sharp breath as the god jerked forward as if pulled by some force within her. His eyes cleared, and he inhaled a deep, rattling gasp, then choked and coughed.

Stunned, Marina scooted away from him, alarmed by

their closeness. Farah was watching her through narrowed eyes.

The god coughed once more, then wiped the spittle from his mouth. "I won't... survive much longer," he rasped. "But the magic of Pandora is spreading. It will take over the other realms."

Farah was shaking her head. "That magic doesn't belong in our world. It will not last."

"Some of it was created specifically *for* your world," the god said, his expression darkening. "There are no limits to what has been unleashed. The magic of the dead will remain with what's left of the Underworld. But anything that *can* cross over will certainly attempt to do so."

Farah's face paled, and Marina scrutinized her. What else besides the kelpies was she so afraid of?

"If you are cursed," Marina said slowly, "then how are you here?" It was clear something was quite wrong with him, but if he'd found a way around his curse, maybe she could do the same.

"I fell through a portal," the god said. "I had no choice. It was either jump in, or be consumed by the dark magic that took over my home."

"So you chose to just die here instead?" Marina asked, overcome by that maddening sense of concern for him once more. *Stop it,* she ordered herself. *You hate him, remember? He can rot for all you care.*

"He will not die," Farah said firmly. "We can help him."

Marina gaped at Farah, and she wasn't the only one.

"Help *him*?" repeated another witch. "This monster from the Underworld? He would spit upon our kind before offering *us* any aid."

Many others shouted their agreement, their voices rising with indignation.

"Have some sense," Farah barked, her eyes flashing. "This death god has magic beyond our own understanding. He alone was able to banish the kelpies. And he alone can track them and locate our sisters. If we help him, he can help us get them back."

"*He* is sitting right here," the god growled.

Farah ignored him and turned to Marina. "You must stay with him, Marina. It's clear you play a key part in breaking through his curse."

Marina blinked. "*Me*?"

"You subdued him. Your touch kept him alive. That can't be a coincidence."

"It *is* a coincidence," Marina insisted. "I'm sure if any one of us had touched him, our fire magic would have awakened him just the same."

"You two are both cursed. I don't know the details or conditions of such a curse, but I know it's binding. It's clear whoever cast it linked you two together somehow. We can use that to find a way to break it."

Break the curse. For a moment, Marina couldn't breathe. Her head was spinning with possibilities.

"You think I haven't already tried to break my curse?" the god growled, still kneeling on the ground. "I've spent hundreds of years using all manner of spells, and nothing has worked. What makes you think *your* magic is any different?"

"Because our magic comes from Hestia herself," Farah said, squaring her shoulders and looking as regal as a queen. "Hestia's magic is the antithesis to Tethys's. If anything can break your curse, it's the power of us fire witches."

The god said nothing. His eyes flashed with a mixture of darkness and longing, a combination Marina only knew too well. She felt her own chest lighten with a dangerous amount of hope. Could her curse truly be broken? And with the very magic that pulsed through her veins?

Farah seemed to interpret the god's silence as agreement. "That settles it, then. We will help each other. So, tell us what we can do. Once we track down the kelpies, how do we destroy them?"

The god was shaking his head, suddenly looking exhausted. His face was drawn and haggard, his dark hair hanging limply around his face. "There's no way to destroy all of them unless we can trap them inside the box again. But the box is in the Underworld, and the

Underworld is…"

"Destroyed," Farah said solemnly. "I see."

"So you're saying we can do nothing," Marina said, her tone flat. "We're just supposed to sit here and wait for these creatures to kill us?"

"There was a time long ago when all magic was freed," Farah said, her eyes distant. "We witches survived then. We can survive it again."

"The kelpies were created by death magic," the god said. "I can track them. I know the scent of it, and my magic will seek it out. If you help me break my curse, I will help you locate the other witches."

Farah nodded stiffly. "Very well. We will set off at once." She straightened and turned toward the witches behind her. "Sisters, prepare yourselves for battle."

"*What?*" Marina shouted, her voice ringing in the cavern. "I—I just got here. I can't go on a journey, and especially not with *him!*" She gestured wildly toward the death god.

"Marina, you're the only one who can keep him alive," Farah said. "We need your help. The offer to break curses extends to you as well. If you help us, we will help you."

Marina was shaking her head, even as every part of her quivered with the anticipation and excitement of living a curse-free life. "I can't leave until I get what I came for."

"And what, exactly, is that?" Farah asked.

Marina opened her mouth, then shut it. She wasn't expecting to expose her deepest desires like this, bluntly and plainly for all to see. But what choice did she have? They already knew about her curse. If the portal was functional, she could abandon these witches right now and jump through, intent on finding Tethys and destroying her.

But right now, she was out of options.

She lifted her chin and tried to put as much confidence into her words as possible. "I was cursed by the goddess Tethys. I came here for information about Hestia, her known enemy, to learn how I can possibly destroy her... along with my curse."

Once more, silence filled the cavern. Even the death god gaped openly at Marina, his face filled with shock.

Farah was watching her with a mixture of confusion and pity as she slowly shook her head. "Marina, how can you possibly hope to take down a goddess? Even if you *did* succeed, this would mean war between us and the gods of Elysium. Is that really what you want?"

"I have been cursed to roam this land for over fifty years," Marina said through clenched teeth. "I have watched family and loved ones die because of the magic ingrained in me. I don't care *what* the consequences are; Tethys overstepped when she cursed me, and I vow to make her pay for that."

"Well, then, the first step would be to track down her creations and destroy them," Farah said, her eyebrows lifting. "You want to find a way to Tethys? Those creatures are the key. It's only a matter of time before the gods get involved in this mess. With darkness roaming the realm once again, the war between Hestia and Tethys has been reignited."

CHAPTER FIVE

THE SANDSTORM HAD LEFT SWIRLING DUNES IN its wake, some lumpy and misshapen, others smooth like hills. Marina gazed solemnly at the crater-sized holes that spotted the ground surrounding the formation of rocks where the witches' cave was hidden. The sun beat down mercilessly from the sky, and she was grateful she was clothed once again so her skin wouldn't burn. With her fair complexion, she'd had enough burns to last a lifetime. Or several lifetimes, in her case.

"The kelpies must draw substance from somewhere," Farah said, appearing next to her and following her gaze. "The sandstorm likely fueled their transformation, making them stronger."

Marina shook her head slowly. "I don't understand

how such creatures can exist. They can die, yes, but they can be reborn? It isn't natural."

"You're right. It isn't. That's part of why they were trapped in Pandora's box in the first place. And why we must venture to put them back. This entire realm is in danger if they remain. Their very existence upsets the balance of power here."

Marina chewed on the inside of her lip but said nothing. For so many years, she had been looking out only for herself. It was hard to spread her awareness to other people; to people who would likely die in a few decades, maybe less, while Marina would continue to wander this dreadful realm. Completely alone.

"We'll cross the desert to the nearest town first," Farah continued. "After that, the death god will show us the way."

Behind them approached several other figures—the last remaining witches of the Rhea coven. Marina's eyes narrowed as she took in the death god, striding alongside Wren, whose head had been bandaged.

"Shouldn't he be tied up?" Marina asked, not bothering to lower her voice.

The god scowled in her direction.

"As long as he keeps his death magic to himself, there is no reason to restrain him," Farah said calmly. "He is our ally until he proves himself otherwise."

Marina wanted to point out that he had already

"accidentally" banished half the coven, thus proving himself to be an enemy. But from the steely look in Farah's eye, she knew it would do no good.

"Stay close to him, Marina," Farah said. "If he starts having fits again, you know what to do."

Marina's face twisted in disgust as she drew one of her daggers, keeping it comfortably in her palm. Farah's eyebrows lifted, but she made no objection. She wrapped her scarf around her face and strode down the rocky path, the other witches following behind her.

After ensuring Wren was well enough to walk without assistance, Marina fell back until she and the death god were walking side-by-side.

He eyed her dagger warily. "Is that truly necessary?"

"If I have to be this close to you, I'm doing it with a dagger in my hand," Marina said without glancing at him. Her eyes were on Wren, who stumbled slightly before righting herself. She needed a healer... but unfortunately, the coven's healer had been whisked away along with the kelpies.

Another thing to blame the death god for.

"I'm not your enemy, Marina," the god said.

Marina flinched at the sound of his voice—not just because it rang with familiarity. But because she *liked* the way her name sounded on his lips. It brought back the intoxicating memories of his body pressed against hers, grinding into her, her back slamming against the stone wall again and again...

Gritting her teeth, she forced the memory from her mind and instead focused on what had happened after.

He'd vanished.

Tethys had appeared.

And Marina's entire life had changed.

"You are hardly my ally," Marina said. "It's because of you I was cursed in the first place."

"You think I wanted that? I was cursed, too. I'm a victim, just like you."

Marina whirled on him, raising the dagger to his throat and hissing through her teeth, "Don't you *dare* claim to be a victim. You are a *god*. You have power and privilege while I remain in this weak and fragile human form, cursed to roam this world alone for all eternity." She cocked her head at him, eyes narrowed. "Tell me, does the throne you sit on sometimes make your ass sore? Do you find your excessive amount of magic burdensome? Are the domains you oversee simply too much to behold?" She scoffed bitterly and spat at his feet. "Spare me your complaints. You will never understand how I have suffered."

His nostrils flared, his jaw tense. The fire in his eyes implied he wanted to argue, but Marina was already turning away from him, dismissing him. For several moments, they traveled across the dunes in silence, following the other witches and tightening the coverings over their faces to protect from the sands and the beating sun above them. Already, Marina's throat ached with a dryness that made her insides feel itchy.

"I do *not* have a throne," the god muttered.

Marina stumbled but righted herself before she fell head first into the sand. "What?" she snapped.

"I do not have a throne," he repeated. "That belongs to my brother, the king of the Underworld."

"Why should I care? Do you expect sympathy?"

"No. But if you are to judge me, you might as well understand the facts before hurling inaccurate insults at me."

Marina clenched her teeth, furious that he had a point. She *didn't* know anything about him. But she also had no desire to. The sooner they used him to locate the kelpies and the other witches, the sooner he could leave her in peace. She wanted nothing more from him.

"My name is Romanos," he said suddenly. "Or Rom, if you prefer."

"I don't care," Marina said at once, even as his name rang in her mind, connecting the missing piece to that elusive masked man from so many years ago. *Romanos.* A powerful name. The name of a god. Perhaps if she'd known his name before their dalliance, she might have hesitated, knowing there was something more to him.

They had just crested the third dune when Rom

suddenly went tense, a strangled groan building up his throat. Marina turned to find him sinking to his knees, his eyes rolling back.

"Dammit." Marina knelt by his side, doubt creeping into her mind as she stretched her hand forward. She felt like an idiot. There was no way Farah was right about this; how could *she*, a cursed fire witch and snake shifter, have any power over this death god?

But when her fingers brushed the strained muscles of his throat, she felt that same shock of awareness rippling through her, binding them together. Rom gasped as if her touch alone had granted him breath, his eyes returning to normal as they fixed on her. His expression was filled with an urgent desperation that made her uncomfortable. He seemed to be pleading with her for something, begging as if she were his deliverance.

Deliverance from *what*?

Marina looked away when his breathing returned to normal, unable to hold that gaze for any longer.

"Thank you," Rom panted, staggering to his feet.

Marina withdrew her hand as if he'd burned her and took a few healthy steps away from him. She said nothing as she turned back to follow the witches, who had lingered when they'd noticed Marina and Rom had fallen behind.

Wren's brow furrowed as she frowned at the pair of them. "Very strange," she muttered.

"Yes, I know," Marina grumbled, falling into step beside her, knowing Rom had at least a little more time before his next episode.

"Do you?" Wren fixed a doubtful look on her. "Do you truly know how strange it is for you to be bound to this death god? Because, to me, it seems like you are in denial."

Marina glared at her. "What do you know about it?"

Wren smirked as if amused she'd struck a nerve. "Not much. But one thing I *do* know is the power of a magical bond. And that's exactly what you two have. The longer you fight it, the more it will pull you together until you have no choice but to face it." She shrugged. "Might as well figure it out now, so you can use it to your advantage. That's what I would do."

Marina had nothing to say to that. Truth be told, she hadn't given it much consideration. Every fiber of her being wanted to distance herself from Rom, to deny any connection they shared because he was her enemy, the reason for her miserable life.

And yet... What if Wren was right? What if there *was* a way Marina could use this to her advantage? Being bound to a god might have its uses... For instance, would it grant her some protection if she were to go after Tethys?

Was this the secret weapon she was looking for?

"Do you have much experience with magical bonds?" Marina asked, noting the dark look that had crossed Wren's face.

Wren's eyes tightened as she kept her gaze fixed straight ahead, but her jaw was taut with tension. "I do."

Marina said nothing for a moment. She was deeply curious, but she didn't want to pry. With an awkward chuckle, she said, "Well, I hope yours wasn't a forced connection to a death god."

Wren huffed a laugh, but it sounded far too bitter. "No. It was by choice. We both consented for the bond to be forged. And then... she died. And it was the worst pain I've ever known. I wouldn't wish it on anyone."

Marina's throat felt tight. She didn't know what to say. The raw agony in Wren's eyes, the pain creasing her expression... She was all too familiar with it. As careful as she'd been all these years, keeping her distance from the world so they wouldn't fall prey to her curse like everyone else—Marina had still made mistakes. People had suffered because of her.

"I'm sorry," Marina said at last. "I know how it feels to lose people close to you. But I can't imagine the strain of losing a bond that powerful." She didn't know much about magical bonds, but from what Remy had told her, they were powerful, volatile, and had the potential to kill whoever was bound. "How did you survive it?"

"Farah helped me." Wren jerked her head toward the coven leader a few paces ahead of them. "I wouldn't have gotten through it without her."

Marina nodded. Though she didn't know Farah well, she knew enough to understand the woman cared for her coven deeply.

"She'll help you, too," Wren said, her eyes shifting to Marina. "If you let her in, she can pull you through your own darkness. Just like she did for me."

Marina's throat turned dry, and she averted her gaze. For a moment, it seemed Wren could see too much of her grief and pain, the losses she kept buried deep so she wouldn't have to relive them over and over again. She didn't want to drag those heavy burdens to the surface. Not now. She didn't have the strength to face them.

And even if she did, she wouldn't dare let Farah in, as Wren had suggested. The very act would turn the coven leader to stone.

So instead, Marina fell silent, allowing the conversation to die before her emotions and her past completely drowned her.

After crossing several more dunes, they climbed to the top of the hill and made out the vast city of Sodara spread out below them. Marina, huffing and exhausted, her throat parched and her skin scratchy, heaved a sigh of relief. Somehow, the journey hadn't seemed so long when she'd made the trek by herself. Then again, she was moving slower with the witches.

And she was constantly aware of Rom's gaze on her, as much as she tried to ignore it.

Farah and the other witches were adjusting their scarves, wrapping them to drape across their foreheads like hoods instead of covering their mouths like before. "Marina, we will need you and... Rom, is it?" She smirked knowingly at the death god, and Marina's cheeks burned with the knowledge that Farah had over-heard their conversation. "We'll need you both to make arrangements for us from here on out. Our eye color will give us away."

"Can't you change it?" Marina asked.

Farah's amber eyes flashed as they drilled into her. "We've been living in isolation for hundreds of years. The entire purpose of our coven was to allow freedom to exist as we are, not as society demands. Those instincts cannot simply be turned off." Her eyes softened. "It is similar to how you cannot fully connect with your shifter side just yet. It takes practice."

Marina dropped her gaze, suddenly self-conscious. It was true she had very little control over her serpent form. And the fact that she couldn't shift without losing her clothing was another obstacle.

Farah grasped her elbow. "We will help you, Marina. You are one of us now."

A lump lodged itself in her throat, and she swallowed hard, her eyes burning. Remy had said something similar to her, often reminding her that the river coven was her family, no matter who she was or where she came from.

Thoughts of Remy flooded her mind. Her body, hard as stone, lying motionless on the bed. The entire village up in flames, burning from Marina's rage and grief.

Marina snatched her arm away quickly. "Thank you," she said, her voice strained. "But you would do well to keep your distance from me. It isn't safe for you. Or anyone." She looked at Wren to ensure she was listening, too. The auburn-haired witch was watching through narrowed eyes, her mouth turned down in contemplation.

"What do you need us to do?" Rom asked, breaking the uncomfortable silence. "Secure a meal and a room for the night?"

Farah nodded and reached into her pack to give him a small sack of coins. "We don't have much, but this should be sufficient."

Marina's skin prickled with suspicion, her eyes on the pouch. Was it truly wise to hand this god their money?

As if reading her apprehension, Rom took the sack and placed it in Marina's hands. She stared up at him in surprise, only to find him smiling at her. "Best if you keep it, I think. I'm likely to drop it if my... condition worsens."

Marina could only gape at him. His eyes crinkled slightly with his warm expression, his mouth twitching as if he found this whole situation amusing. She had never seen such a gentle look on his face before. It completely transformed him from the terrifying death god into someone kind and affectionate. A perfect stranger.

She was reminded of the man with the fox mask. He hadn't looked at her with such tenderness—their interactions had been feral and carnal, pleasure-seeking and nothing more. But the expression he wore here and now brought her back to that feeling of warmth and understanding she'd experienced for the briefest of moments while their bodies collided.

I'll never feel that fulfilled again.

Those were her exact thoughts after he'd taken her against the wall. At the time, she'd been thinking of the physical sensation, the way his body had completely filled hers, satisfying her in a way no man ever had before.

But no, she'd felt something deeper with him. Something else. Something she couldn't quite name. As much as she didn't want to admit it, since she'd spent so many years despising him, that moment *had* been different from any ordinary lovers' tryst.

"There is an inn at the bottom of the hill," Farah said, snapping Marina from her hazy thoughts. "We've stayed there before, and the innkeeper is very discreet."

"Does he know you're fire witches?" Rom asked.

Farah offered a bitter smile. "No. But he is no fool. He knows we're hiding something and would like to keep it hidden. We'll stay there for the night and continue with our journey at dawn." She paused, scrutinizing Rom. "You said you're able to track the kelpies. Do you know where they reside now?"

Rom shook his head. "I'll need to cast a spell and summon my death magic. It's a dangerous task, and any creature of magic nearby will scent it. I'm drawn to them, and they are drawn to me. Best to only cast it when we are ready to flee, so we can try to outrun whatever might be lurking nearby."

Marina suppressed a shudder as she imagined more demon horses springing up from the ground.

With Farah leading the way, they skirted downhill, their footsteps a light shuffle to avoid tumbling down the dune. Marina's foot dragged in the sand, and she staggered before someone caught her arm, steadying her.

"Thanks," she said, only to realize it was Rom who grasped her. She jerked free of his grip, scowling, as they continued downhill. She could've sworn he chuckled in response.

As they descended, the sandy ground became rockier

and sturdier, their footsteps now making loud scuffling sounds instead of the gentle whisper among the dunes. Marina resisted the urge to wrap her scarf more securely around herself to hide from passersby. It was instinct to draw as little attention to herself as possible.

But with the other witches' need to remain obscured, it was imperative that Marina leave her face uncovered. A crowd of masked witches was suspicious. But if two of them bore their faces for the world to see? It would be less conspicuous. She shared a glance with Rom, who lifted his chin, his stride a confident swagger that made him look like he belonged. Watching him only made Marina's scowl deepen as she thought of her own clumsy shuffling, her body hunched over from years of keeping her face lowered to avoid meeting other people's eye. She tried to emulate his confidence, throwing her shoulders back and raising her face. The back of her neck prickled even though she knew no one was following them. The small buildings on the outer edge of the village drew closer. A few townspeople were out and about, meandering along the sandy roads. Some of them cast curious glances Marina's way, but she forced herself to meet their gazes and incline her head politely.

To her surprise, they returned the gesture before resuming their activities. Marina struggled to breathe properly, waiting for the moment when someone would point at her and scream, or a man would look at her with lust in his eyes. Her pale skin and green eyes often attracted unwanted attention, and when it didn't, the fire magic roiling inside her did. Sometimes her eyes would flash amber without her permission.

Rom nudged her gently. "You're all right," he murmured.

She glared at him. "What are you talking about?"

"You seem uneasy. I know you're accustomed to being hunted, but these people don't suspect anything."

"Yet," Marina grumbled.

Rom grinned. "Keep your suspicions about you. It's good to assume the worst, to prepare for things to go awry. But don't let it make you paranoid."

Marina gritted her teeth. "I'm sorry, are you *lecturing* me right now?"

"Just offering some tips."

"From what, your vast experience of blending in with crowds and avoiding brutal attacks?" Marina scoffed. "Spare me. You've probably never been hunted a day in your life."

Rom's eyes darkened. "You don't know much about the Underworld, do you?"

Marina blinked, startled by the question. "What?"

"Do you know what I was tasked with for so many years?" His eyes were lethal as he stared at her. All Marina could do was shake her head. "I was in charge of guarding Tartarus."

A knot of dread formed in Marina's chest. *Tartarus.* Rom was right; she *didn't* know much about the Underworld. But what she did know was that Tartarus was a prison for the most vile of souls. It preyed on their fears and turned their minds against them. It enslaved their minds as well as their bodies.

Even if Rom wasn't technically a prisoner, Marina couldn't imagine how he would survive that place for long without it affecting him.

Shame and confusion swirled in her mind as she processed this. Was she feeling... *sympathy* for this god who had ruined her life? It was so sudden and unexpected, and yet, she couldn't deny that she had—once again—completely misjudged him.

With a brisk shake of her head, she muttered, "Sorry. I didn't know."

"That's all right." Rom's amused smile returned, and this somehow made her angry all over again.

Intent on fully understanding him—just so she could feel justified in despising him, she told herself—Marina asked, "Were you—I mean, did Tartarus—Was your life ever in danger down there?"

Rom's expression sobered, his gaze turning distant. "I was never in any danger. But oftentimes, my mind believed I was. That place plays tricks on you, and once it lures you in, it's already won. It only takes one deception for the illusion to solidify in your mind and claim you completely."

Marina's blood ran cold. "Goddess," she breathed. "That sounds terrible."

"It is."

"Why were you tasked with that? Couldn't you work somewhere else?"

Rom offered a wry smile. "I didn't have much control over that. As I've told you, my brother rules the Underworld. The assignments are up to him."

There was a lilt to his tone that made Marina watch him closely. His eyes were guarded, and he wouldn't look at her.

"It's more than that, though," she said quietly. "Isn't it?"

Rom's eyebrows lifted. "I—Well..." He sighed. "Yes. By working in Tartarus, I was able to avoid many of my brothers."

"You have more than one?"

"Oh yes. I have five. Well, four. One of them perished. But many of them are just as vile as the depths of Tartarus. If they had known about my curse, they would have used it against me."

Marina's brow furrowed. "One of your brothers perished? A *god*? How?"

Rom snorted and shot her a dubious look. "Why? You considering doing the same to me?"

Marina's head reared back. "I—" Actually, she had been thinking of Tethys.

Rom, caught off guard by her confusion, smoothed his expression. "He was killed by my brother. Another god." He looked at her pointedly as if to say, *No mortal can kill a god.*

Marina said nothing. Her head was full of strange, incoherent thoughts of gods and Tartarus and Romanos, the death god who was responsible for her curse, living a life of torment and despair in the Underworld. It clashed with everything she'd believed for so many years, picturing him enjoying a life of frivolity and endless pleasures with all the other gods.

But it was far more complicated than that.

And she was starting to wonder if, perhaps, Rom's life had been even more miserable than hers.

CHAPTER SIX

WHEN THEY REACHED THE INN, FARAH AND THE other witches elected to wait outside while Marina and Rom purchased the room. Farah gave them explicit instructions on what to say to the innkeeper. Once the transaction was complete, the witches would slip through the back to access the room.

It all seemed very covert and incredibly likely to fail, in Marina's opinion. From her experience, it was better to appear as ordinary and unassuming as possible, and this plan was the complete opposite.

But, in spite of her concerns, she trusted Farah. And, if all else failed, every single one of them possessed powerful magic. They could defend themselves if needed.

Squaring her shoulders, Marina followed Rom into

the small inn. They stepped into a tiny pub filled with only a few occupants drinking ale in the corner. Behind the bar was a short man with no hair and a faint white goatee along his chin. He adjusted his spectacles when they approached.

This was the innkeeper Farah had described. *So far, so good,* Marina thought.

She lifted her chin and set the pouch of coins down on the bar. "We'd like a meal and a room for the night, please." She leaned forward. "And we are willing to pay for your discretion as well. We are friends of Felicity's."

The man, who was watching with narrowed eyes, now straightened at the usage of Farah's alias. His eyes widened, and he nodded fervently. "Ah, I see. I was wondering when we might see our elusive friend again. Is she well?"

In an undertone, Marina said, "She is. And she's here with us now. We would appreciate the usage of your backdoor if possible. She has brought others with her who also require discretion."

The man arched an eyebrow as he started counting the coins in the pouch. "That will cost you extra."

Marina nodded. "Of course." She tried to appear confident, even though she worried their funds wouldn't be enough. Farah certainly didn't have much, but they needed a place to stay. After a long day traveling in the desert, they needed food and rest, especially if what Rom spoke was true, and dark magical creatures would be hunting them soon.

When the innkeeper was satisfied the coins were the right amount, he slid them back into the pouch, then turned and swiped a key hanging on a hook along the wall behind him. He jerked his head toward the back. "Follow me. I'll let your friends in."

Relief filled Marina's chest. "Thank you."

The innkeeper led them through the back and down a cluttered hallway filled with crates and jugs of ale. When he opened the door, Farah was waiting on the other side with a smile.

"Bernard! It's been too long." To Marina's surprise, Farah embraced the innkeeper, who chuckled slightly.

"I was starting to worry something had happened to you," he said gruffly when they drew apart.

"No, I just needed to lie low. Too much time in town draws unwanted attention."

Bernard nodded. "Of course, of course. Well, you know you're welcome here anytime." He passed her the room key and glanced uncertainly over her shoulder. Marina could see his mind working as he tallied up how many guests would be sharing one room.

Farah took the key before he could probe her with questions. Already, Marina was shifting uncomfortably at the idea of sharing a room with this many people—including Rom. She likely wouldn't sleep at all.

"Thank you, Bernard." Farah smiled warmly at him. "And should you or your family need any, ah, *assistance* while I'm here, please let me know."

Bernard's cheeks reddened, and he cleared his throat and rubbed his nose. "Ah, yes. Of course." He opened his mouth as if to say something else, then thought better of it and turned and shuffled down the hallway.

Marina frowned after him. She was about to ask Farah what that had been about, but the coven leader pressed a finger to her lips and shook her head. Together, Marina, Rom, and the fire witches crept up the stairs to the rooms. Farah must have stayed in this particular room before, because she seemed to know exactly where she was going. It was the first door on the left, and Marina understood why it was so appealing: it was closest to the staircase, just in case they needed to flee quickly.

Farah unlocked the door and let everyone inside. The room was small, filled with a single, narrow bed with a stack of quilts at the foot. A small table with a pitcher of water rested next to the bed.

Marina immediately went to the window and drew the curtain, but not before she got a clear view of the dunes they had left behind. As soon as the door was closed, she asked, "So, what's this arrangement you have with Bernard?"

Farah sighed as she removed the covering from her

face. Several other witches sat on the floor and did the same, some stretching their legs, and others resting their heads against the wall. "He has a daughter who is showing early signs of magic. We aren't certain which kind yet. But I've been seeing her, assessing her abilities, and giving her enchantments to keep her gifts hidden for now."

Marina's eyes widened. "A witch? From non-magical parents?"

Farah nodded gravely. "I suspect there was a witch somewhere in the wife's bloodline, though she refuses to talk about it. At any rate, Bernard is worried word will spread about his daughter and he'll lose the business he's built here."

"What will happen when they can't hide her powers any longer?" Marina asked.

"Then Bernard will have to make the difficult decision to either send her away to a coven for training, or expose her to the village."

Marina shook her head in frustration. Very few places fully accepted witches and the magic they practiced. It was one of the reasons why covens often lived in isolation. She had no doubt that if the people here knew of Bernard's daughter, they would react with fear—and possibly violence.

Marina had experienced this firsthand when she couldn't rein in her fire magic.

"Wren, you take the bed," Farah said. "The rest of us will find a spot on the floor." She started sifting through the pile of quilts, laying them side-by-side along the floorboards.

Wren didn't object, which only added to Marina's concerns. The auburn-haired witch sank onto the bed with a groan, her hand lifting to her forehead. Patches of blood had seeped through the bandage.

Marina strode forward, reaching into her bag for spare bandages before kneeling at the bedside. "Let me change those for you."

Wren looked at her skeptically. "Have you any healing experience?"

Marina snorted. "Just the essentials to stay alive. But I know enough to know that when your bandage is bleeding through, it needs to be replaced."

Wren nodded once, her jaw stiff, as Marina carefully unraveled the wrappings that covered her wound.

It was worse than Marina expected. She'd anticipated a shallow gash, but this looked like a chunk of her scalp had been torn clean off, leaving a wide, bloody expanse across the left side of her head. Patches of her hair had been ripped away.

Marina swallowed down bile, trying to keep her expression neutral as she pulled out a healing balm to dab at the wound.

But Wren saw right through her. "I know. It's bad."

"We just need to get you to a proper healer. That's all."

"Not an ordinary healer. This injury was inflicted by dark magic. Only someone familiar with this particular brand of magic can reverse its effects."

Marina met her gaze. Wren's lips had thinned, her expression grim. "It's spreading," she whispered. "Soon it will cover my entire scalp. Then spread to the rest of my face until it kills me."

Marina's heart jolted. "How do you know this?"

"Farah told me. She wanted me to know the extent of the injury. It wasn't just a strike from the kelpie; it was infused with their magic. The same magic in Pandora's box."

Horror crept up Marina's throat. Goddess, if the kelpies were capable of that, then they were in more trouble than she'd thought.

Wren gripped her wrist, her face filled with urgency. "I'm telling you this to *warn* you. I saw you rush at those kelpies with no thought for yourself. But what if they infect you, too?"

Marina squeezed her hand. "Don't worry about me, Wren. My—My curse keeps me alive. No matter what injuries I'm dealt."

Wren's brow furrowed. "That's even worse. If you are doomed to live through every wound and infection, then this will only keep spreading through your body. It isn't something you can heal from naturally. You will *become* one of those dark creatures, Marina."

Marina stared at her, her blood icing over with the realization that she was right. Every mortal wound she'd suffered from had either healed on its own, or remained in her body until she could find a proper healer. Nothing had ever magically disappeared, even after it had taken her past death's door. She simply... remained alive. Never dying.

Marina finished cleaning and wrapping Wren's wound in complete silence, her heart twisting with sympathy and rage that this had happened to her friend. When she finished, she glanced over her shoulder to find Rom standing nearby, arms crossed as he watched her with darkness roiling in his gaze. The other witches were busy positioning themselves on the floor, preparing to sleep, but it was clear Rom had been listening to their conversation.

"Can you help her?" Marina asked. "Your magic is connected to the kelpies... Maybe—"

But Rom shook his head. "Even if my magic were strong enough—and in this realm, it isn't—I'm no healer. A wound this complicated needs a healer's understanding of the mortal body and how the muscles and tissues are connected." Sorrow filled his eyes. "I'm sorry."

Wren said nothing, her expression blank as if she'd

expected this answer. Without another word, she lay back on the bed, wincing in pain as her head hit the pillow.

Marina stood, arms crossed, as she turned to face Rom. "Bastard," she muttered.

Rom's head reared back. "What?"

"You won't even *try*! She's sick, Rom. And your magic might be the only thing that can save her."

"Or it could mutate her into something worse. Something *darker.* Go on, ask her which she would prefer—to die a clean death, or to become possessed by my death magic. She'll join those kelpies and turn on you."

Marina clenched her teeth, nostrils flaring. Deep down, she knew he was right. But it was so easy to hate him, to pin the blame on *him* for this situation.

"You called me Rom," he said suddenly.

Her eyes snapped to his, and she glared. "So?"

A slow smile spread across his face. "You've just... never said my name before."

Heat and anger mingled in her chest. She was torn between hiding her face from him and punching him in the throat. "I can always just call you *asshole.* Or *bastard.* I feel like those suit you better."

Rom laughed. "Maybe they do."

In spite of herself, Marina found her mouth twitching, an easy smile ready to spread across her lips. Before it could, she turned away from him and said over her shoulder, "I'll be by the window. You'd better be close by or else your curse might take you in your sleep." She shot him a lethal smile. "And what a shame that would be, to wake up and find you dead."

To her surprise, his grin only widened. "Yes. Such a shame. I'm sure you would weep openly at my funeral."

Marina snorted, unable to hide her smile as she snatched a quilt and spread it along the floor by the window.

CHAPTER SEVEN

MARINA DREAMED OF A MAN SHE'D MET IN THE marketplace twenty years ago. He had been watching her haggling for some fruit. When the merchant had dismissed her, spitting at her feet, the man had stepped in, offering his own money to pay for it.

At the time, Marina had been torn between irritation and gratitude. When she'd insisted on paying the man back, he grinned slyly at her and told her she could repay him by joining him for dinner.

In another time and place, Marina would have said no. She would have distanced herself from this man as much as possible, to protect both herself and him.

But she was so very lonely. And her curse hadn't claimed anyone in years. Perhaps, just this once, it would be safe.

They dined. Afterwards, he brought her to his room and took her to bed with such raw, animal passion that Marina's blood boiled, her insides thrumming with an energy she never knew she lacked. He made love to her thoroughly. Beautifully. He made her cry out in ecstasy and delight, experiencing that peak of pleasure she'd been missing for so long.

But even at her climax, when release shattered through her, all she could think of was that mysterious god, how he had wrung her out like a wet cloth, how he had elicited a combination of desperation and satisfaction in a way she had never experienced before. He had filled her completely. And this new man, this stranger, while his body was pleasant and warm and could still make her feel things she yearned for... It wasn't the same.

I'll never feel that fulfilled again.

When Marina woke, the man from the marketplace had been turned to stone, his eyes closed, his body curled against hers, cold and rock-hard, never to breathe or touch again.

The sight of him, dead and frozen because of *her,* had broken Marina completely.

That had been the last time she'd taken a man to her bed. For years after that, she'd had to find pleasure in her own way—never as satisfying, but enough to meet her needs.

As Marina dreamed about this man, the vision shifted. When she awoke, he had turned to stone... but it wasn't the man's kind face she saw.

It was Rom's. He wore his fox mask, a smirk lighting up his face, his entire body now made of stone.

Because of her.

Marina jolted awake with a gasp, her heart hammering madly in her chest. Cold sweat clung to her skin as she sat up, rubbing the back of her neck and trying to wipe the memory of Rom's lifeless body from her mind.

Why did she care? Why did that image frighten her so? It would be poetic justice for him to be turned to stone. After all, he was at fault for her curse. It was only fitting.

Marina smoothed her damp hair from her sweaty face, shivering from the intensity of her vivid nightmare. She often dreamed of them—the people she'd killed with her carelessness. Remy. Giselle. All the witches from the coven who had raised her. The men she'd bedded out of ignorance, thinking surely Tethys wouldn't deprive her of *all* companionship. Any stranger who might have cared too much for her, taken pity and shown affection and love for her when she'd been in need.

Tears burned behind her eyes, and she clenched her teeth, determined not to drown in the agony that threatened to consume her. Most nights, she could push such thoughts from her mind.

But not tonight. Not when Rom was nearby, reminding her of everything she'd lost and why.

She shot a glance toward him. He was wrapped up in a quilt, his body tucked toward the wall and away from her. His shoulders rose and fell with the steady breathing of sleep. She wasn't sure if she was more relieved to find him getting some rest, or annoyed that he wasn't lying awake, haunted by his curse just like she was.

With a shake of her head, Marina sat up, her gaze drifting over the sleeping forms of the witches around her. Desperate to take her mind off her past horrors, she lifted a hand and tried summoning her flames. The fire magic burned within her, churning restlessly, but when she tried to conjure fire with just one hand, nothing happened. Marina scowled, flexing her fingers, pouring all her focus into one small tendril of flame.

But her magic raged and thrashed inside her, almost as if it were too angry to comply with her wishes. Her powers were too volatile. She could either summon it *all* and set herself on fire, or summon nothing at all.

Marina let her hand fall with a huff of frustration, then jumped when someone spoke.

"You've shackled your magic for too long."

The voice, while soft, pierced through the silence of the night, making Marina's heart race all over again. Her eyes scanned the room until she found one of the witches—a dark-haired woman named Dahlia—sitting up with her back against the wall.

"I've been watching you since we left," she went on. "You see your magic as something dangerous to be contained. You are too afraid of it. You must treat it as an equal partner who shares your body. Who has needs, just as you do. It isn't your enemy, but your ally."

Marina shook her head. "My magic isn't to be trusted. It kills without reason. If I relinquish control—"

"It isn't about relinquishing control. It's about letting your magic breathe freely." Dahlia paused, her mouth turning down in contemplation. "I'm a teacher, charged with training other witches. For years, I've worked on educating our people in our histories, ensuring the past generations are not forgotten, as well as exercising our abilities to keep them active and controlled. I've seen witches like you, Marina, who bury their magic down deep. Fear makes you ignorant. And if you were my pupil, my first lesson would be to accept and embrace the side of magic that frightens you so. *You* are still present, Marina. It is still *your* body. You are merely allowing your magic to borrow it. If you cage it, it will fester and fight against you, seeing you as the enemy. But if you show it respect and understanding, if you meet its needs and set it loose, then you will find that equilibrium and balance."

Marina wasn't convinced. "Say I'm in a public place when my magic wishes to be set free. What do I do then?"

Dahlia offered a wry smile. "Ah. That is the benefit of living in isolation. When our serpents and flames call for us, we can answer at any time. But, amongst humans, it can be difficult to find that balance. In time, you will develop a rhythm with your magic, anticipating when it needs to be unleashed before it happens. For instance, my serpent must be released every forty-eight hours, down to the exact minute. If you choose to live among the humans, this is something you can prepare for. Find a private space to free your magic, somewhere away from prying eyes and witnesses."

A hard knot of emotion formed in Marina's throat. *If you choose to live among humans.* She said it so simply, as if Marina had a choice of lifestyle. As if there was a happy ending for her after this.

But no. Once Marina found a way to break her curse, she would be going after Tethys. And she had no expectations of surviving the encounter.

In fact, she welcomed death. It was long overdue for her.

Reminded of her curse, Marina turned away from Dahlia, fixing her gaze on a loose thread of her quilt. "You shouldn't talk to me."

To her surprise, Dahlia chuckled. "Why? You think your curse will claim me?"

"Well... yes."

"Who cursed you?"

Marina shot her a dark look. "You know who."

"Humor me."

Marina sighed. "Tethys."

"And who is Tethys's greatest enemy?"

Frowning, Marina said slowly, "Hestia."

"Yes. Hestia blessed the Rhea coven with the powers of her Gorgon sisters. In the war against Tethys and Neptune, Hestia needed a way to imbue her followers with something that was immune to water magic. The power flowing in my blood is the antidote to your curse, Marina."

Marina's insides froze in shock as if she herself had been turned to stone. "You can't know that for sure." Her voice was hushed as she dared to hope.

"I can. I'm a teacher, remember? No one is as well-versed in our history as I am. Tales from centuries ago indicate that Hestia's blood has curse-breaking abilities."

Marina's heart lurched. "Curse-breaking? Do you think that's the key to undoing my curse?"

"I do. But I don't think it's as simple as that. If the key is in your blood, then that means only *you* have the power to undo the curse."

Marina suppressed a groan. "Don't you think that if

it was in my power to end my curse, I would have done it already?"

"Of course. But curses are far more complicated than that. For instance, what if the key to breaking the curse is the same barrier that's holding you back from your fire magic? What if embracing that side of yourself is the key?"

Marina fell silent at that. It would be just like Tethys to curse Marina and make the solution so obvious and yet so unattainable. For how could Marina embrace the very powers that made her a monster, that made her hunted, an abomination to be feared?

"Could it really be that easy?" Marina whispered.

Dahlia huffed a laugh. "Easy? Bonding with your serpent and embracing your fire magic is not easy. I know that firsthand from training new witches. But I can help you through it. I'd be glad to be your tutor."

Marina shook her head. "I still think it's a bad idea. Every time I get close to someone…" She trailed off, her eyes burning with the memories of all she'd lost.

"It's far too late for that. Because I began to care for you the instant you shifted into a serpent and attacked those kelpies to save my sisters. I know I'm not the only one."

Marina shut her eyes against the onslaught of emotions tunneling through her. Grief and regret that Dahlia would have been turned to stone so soon after meeting her. Comfort and gratitude that these witches could look on her with affection and kindness, even after knowing what she was capable of.

A desperate sense of inadequacy, because surely she didn't deserve it. Not one bit.

"Do you truly believe your coven is immune?" Marina asked, her voice barely above a breath. Could there really be a loophole to Tethys's curse? Could she really find companionship with these witches? She knew better than to hope... After all this time, hope was a dangerous thing. And it crushed her every time. And yet, she couldn't help that blossoming feeling from spreading within her.

"It was something I speculated as soon as I heard of your involvement with Tethys," Dahlia said. "But I wasn't certain until I heard you speaking with Rom about your curse."

Marina's cheeks burned, and she couldn't help but shoot another glare toward Rom. He had shifted to lie on his back, eyes closed and one hand resting on his abdomen as he slept.

"When all this is over," Dahlia said, "you will have a place with us, if it's what you want. I know Farah would welcome you. Hestia's power runs through your veins as well."

Marina had to close her eyes as a shuddering breath rocked her body. A coven. A *family.* How long had she yearned for such a thing, never daring to hope she could experience that kind of love ever again?

"Do you really think," Marina said in a choked voice, blinking tears from her eyes, "that I have the power to break this curse myself?"

Dahlia was silent for a long moment. After a while, she said, "I do not know anything for certain. But I speculate your curse is connected to your magic... and this death god. I don't think it's a coincidence that your touch affects him. It's clear you have some kind of bond or connection that is tethered to the curse. But Tethys built her spell in a way I do not recognize, with magic and powers I am unfamiliar with. She has... grown in her abilities. Which does not bode well for us. If she no longer needs the dark magic of Pandora to come after our people, then we are in grave danger indeed."

A solemn silence fell between them, broken only by the heavy breathing of the witches around them.

With a shout, Rom jerked upright into a sitting position, his spine stiff and his body going rigid. He uttered the same choking, gasping noises as before, and Marina sighed heavily as she scooted closer to him, prepared to subdue him with her touch.

But this time, something was different. He spread his arms, his head thrown back, the muscles and veins taut against his skin. His whole body started to quiver and convulse.

Marina hurried over to him, placing herself in front of him and resting her hands on his cheeks. "Rom? *Rom*!"

He didn't respond. His eyes rolled back so they were all white. Foam spread across his lips. And along his arms were long, inky vines crawling up his skin, wrapping around him like cords.

Marina looked up to find Farah rising from the floor, her face alert as if she hadn't slept at all. "Farah! What's wrong with him?"

Farah was by her side in an instant, her hands on Rom's shoulders. Black was creeping into his eyes. "Death magic," she murmured, closing her eyes as she pressed her fingertips to his temples. "I can't reach him. He is trapped by magic not of this realm."

Marina shook his shoulders. "*Rom*! Wake up!"

A few witches stirred from her shouting, but she paid them no attention. Rom was dying. And without him, they couldn't locate the kelpies or the other witches.

He couldn't die. Marina wouldn't allow it.

She released his shoulders and slapped him hard across the face. His head swiveled from the impact, and he let out a choked gag as he coughed on the foam rising up his throat. Marina pressed her hands against his chest and summoned her fire magic.

All of it.

As if sensing what she was about to do, Farah threw her hands in the air and muttered, *"Protego."*

Just as Marina's body erupted in flames, an orange dome surrounded her and Rom, protecting the rest of the room from her fire. Marina pressed her palms harder against Rom's chest, pouring her fire magic into him. He jerked and spasmed against her, but she held fast. If his curse was connected to *her*, well, then, she would boil the death magic right out of him.

A strangled cry burst from his lips, growing in intensity until he was screaming and thrashing with pain. The smell of burned flesh met Marina's nose, but she kept her grip on him, feeding him more and more of her flames, praying it wouldn't kill him, that his god blood would protect him...

"Marina!" he cried out. *"Marina!"* Her name was a desperate plea, and it sounded so personal and intimate that Marina's skin turned ice cold, despite the flames licking her skin. She released him abruptly, and her fire magic vanished, plunging the room into darkness once more.

Rom fell forward, and Marina barely caught him before his head hit the floor. He was gasping for breath and trembling, his body covered in sweat. His skin burned against hers. As she righted him, she noticed a scorching hole had burned through his shirt, exposing the bare skin of his chest. Thankfully, his skin was unmarred, and Marina loosed a breath of relief.

"Gods," he groaned, eyes shut, face contorted with pain. "What the hell *was* that?"

"Your death magic," Farah said, waving her hands to disperse the protective dome surrounding them. "From the curse. It must have a stronger hold on you than we'd thought. It's calling you back to the Underworld."

Rom was gasping for breath, still leaning heavily on Marina. She looked up at Farah. "What can we do?"

"We can move onward," Farah said, striding across the room and rousing the few witches who had slept through the ordeal. "*Now.*"

Marina's eyes widened. "Now? In the dead of night?" It wouldn't be the first time she'd traveled this way, but it still startled her, the notion of several fire witches and a death god skulking through the city in the middle of the night.

"Yes." With the witches awake, Farah was gathering the quilts and placing them at the foot of the bed again. "He unleashed quite a powerful dose of death magic. Creatures will come sniffing around. We haven't much time."

"She's right," Rom said, his voice a weak rasp. "I can sense dark creatures nearby. They're drawing closer."

Marina was on her feet in an instant. She went to the bed to help Wren dress. The other witches were scrambling around the room, collecting belongings and conjuring protective spells.

When everyone was ready, Farah opened the door, ushering the witches through. Marina guided Wren through the doorway with Rom behind them.

Just before the door shut, something exploded through the window, spraying shattered glass across the floor.

CHAPTER EIGHT

MARINA FROZE IN THE DOORWAY, TORN BETWEEN flying down the stairs with the other witches and facing the creature before her. Terror iced her over, rendering her motionless as the monster stalked forward.

It was a lion... with three heads. The head of a lion, the head of a goat, and the head of a serpent. At the sight of the snake head, Marina's fire magic churned inside her, eager to be unleashed.

Okay, Dahlia, Marina thought warily, *let's try this your way.*

She let loose her magic. Her body exploded into flames, and she swore she felt an inward sigh of relief from the serpent inside her. Her body shifted and elongated, white scales sprouting along her skin. She hissed loudly, uncoiling and creeping toward the creature.

"Marina!" Rom shouted.

Marina faltered for a moment, not realizing Rom had lingered with her. She turned her serpent's head toward him, trying to convey the urgency of the situation. She jerked her head toward the hall and then toward the three-headed creature.

Understanding lit Rom's face. He glanced down the hall as well, his gaze roving over the closed doors of the other occupants.

There were innocent people here. If Marina fled with the other witches, where would this creature go? What havoc would it wreak? Who would it kill in its path to the witches?

No, Marina had to end it here and now. Before anyone else got hurt.

To her surprise, Rom stood by her side, hands spread wide and black smoke pooling from his fingertips. He gave her a sure nod as they advanced toward the monster.

Marina vaguely recognized it from the ancient texts she had studied over the years. It was a chimera, a fire-breathing hybrid creature. But as Marina inched closer, she realized she was not afraid. It breathed fire? Well, she was born of fire. It had three heads? One of those was a snake, and it was pitiful compared to her own serpent.

The remaining heads she knew she could handle.

Go ahead, she challenged it. *Come for me. See what happens when you try.*

The lion head growled as it prowled closer, its paws thudding against the floorboards. When it lunged, Marina was ready for it. The lion's body was powerful, but Marina was quick and lithe. She slithered out of the way, narrowly avoiding the sharpened claws of the beast. Rom hit the creature with a burst of his death magic as Marina coiled around its middle, sinking her fangs into its hide.

The creature roared, the sound unearthly and demonic with the layered cries of each animal. The serpent head nudged toward Marina, fangs extended, but Marina dodged its strike, biting the snake neck until she tasted blood.

The snake head fell limply against the lion's body.

Fire burst from the lion's jaws, but Marina's body was impervious to it. The flames did nothing to her. She wrapped her long body around the lion's throat. It clawed at her, cutting through her scales, carving a path of fire and agony down her body, but she held fast. Rom roared with rage and dived forward, tackling the lion to the floor and taking Marina with it. She tightened her hold on the lion's throat as Rom grappled with it, keeping those claws busy as she squeezed and squeezed and squeezed...

The lion's movements slowed, and a low whine rumbled from its throat before it slumped over.

All that remained was the goat head. Its dark eyes appraised Marina and Rom with uncertainty. It looked almost comical, this lifeless lion body and snake head lying on the floor with nothing but the head of a goat left to defend itself. It seemed the torso and legs were connected to the lion's head, which was rendered unconscious. So, what could the goat do?

The goat seemed to realize this, bowing its head in submission. Marina loosened her hold on the lion's throat and slithered to the floor. But Rom was still glaring at the creature. In one swift movement, he grasped the goat's neck and twisted. A loud *crack* echoed in the room as the creature fell, dead. For good measure, Rom snapped the lion's neck as well, though this took more effort.

Marina cringed inwardly, recalling the goat's shrewd gaze. It had surrendered to them. It had chosen to live rather than to keep fighting.

And Rom still took its life.

Marina let her head droop, emitting a low, sorrowful hiss.

Rom seemed to understand her as if she'd spoken aloud. "It would have kept hunting us," he said gruffly, wiping sweat from his brow. "You know this, Marina."

She did. She forced the thoughts from her mind as she shifted back to her human form.

"Shit." Rom's eyes went wide, his gaze flicking over her naked form before he quickly turned away. "Get some clothes on, Marina."

"I can't exactly control it," she snapped, grabbing her pile of clothes that lay abandoned in the corner. The long gashes from the lion's claws marred her skin, leaving trails of blood down her side. With a groan, she struggled to don the shirt and trousers without fainting from the pain, her flesh burning with each movement. She would certainly need to get her injuries looked at.

But not now. Now, they had to run before more creatures tracked them down.

After hastily dressing, she and Rom hurried down the stairs and out the backdoor, rejoining the other witches.

"Thank the Goddess." Farah embraced her at once, her face full of devastation and regret. "I wanted to turn back and help, but I couldn't. Wren..." She turned, and Marina's heart leapt in her throat.

Sitting on a barrel, her face covered in blood, was Wren, rocking back and forth and muttering to herself. Three witches surrounded her, trying in vain to calm her, but their presence only seemed to agitate her further.

"What happened to her?" Marina whispered.

"The arrival of the demon triggered it," Dahlia said gravely as she rubbed Wren's arms. "I think there's something in Pandora's magic that activates whatever she was poisoned with when it draws near."

Poisoned. Goddess, did that mean that Wren was... dying?

Wren moaned and clawed at her bandages, drawing more scratches down her scalp that bled freely. She was reopening her wounds.

Marina was by her side in an instant, hissing in pain as the slashes along her side throbbed. Ignoring her injuries, she took Wren's hands in hers. "Wren, look at me. Please."

Wren's amber eyes flitted back and forth, not seeing Marina at all. Her face was ghostly pale, all traces of her usual amusing smirk now gone.

"*Wren.*" Marina pressed her palms against Wren's cheeks. Her insides burned, the flames inside her igniting, and for the second time that evening, she let them loose—one tendril of flame at a time. Fire scorched her fingertips, burning into Wren's skin. Wren yelped, jerking violently as Marina quickly withdrew her hands before she melted the witch's flesh.

Several red, blistering marks appeared on Wren's cheeks, and she swore loudly, eyes shut tight and her face scrunched up in pain. "Burning, bleeding, *hell*, Marina! What was that for?"

A surprised laugh bubbled up in Marina's throat, tinged with relief. It had worked. Wren was back. Several witches hurried forward to tend to Wren's fresh wounds, and Farah looked on with a mixture of shock and gratitude.

"Sorry," Marina said, still chuckling. Hysterical tears tickled her eyes, and she let them fall, too exhausted and pained to wipe them away. "You were gone. I needed a way to bring you back."

"You channeled your fire into a smaller scope," Farah said in amazement. "Well done, Marina."

Marina swallowed and averted her gaze, suddenly uncomfortable. "Thanks."

Once Wren's wounds were re-bandaged, three witches helped her to her feet, and Farah announced, "We're leaving now. Before we bring any other creatures here."

"Marina, you need to get that looked at." Rom, who had remained quiet until now, gestured to Marina's side. Blood was leaking through her clothes, making the fabric cling to her torn flesh.

Marina was about to snap at him, but she clutched at her side as a fresh stab of pain ripped through her. Darkness crept into her vision, and she slumped against one of the barrels.

"Why didn't you say anything?" Farah demanded, hurrying forward to examine her wounds. She inhaled a breath through her teeth as she inspected it. "This will need stitches."

"We don't have time for that," Marina argued through clenched teeth. "Rom used his magic up there. More creatures will be coming."

"If I don't stitch this up now, you'll bleed out on the road."

"I *can't die*," Marina bit out. "Just carry my body as far as you can go."

"We'll travel twice as slowly with your dead weight," Farah said sharply.

"I can carry her," Rom said at once.

"*No*," Marina argued, though she had no idea why; as the only male—and a muscular one at that—he was clearly the best choice.

"I can keep up with your pace, even with her weight," Rom went on. "And if my curse tries to claim me, she'll be able to calm me immediately."

Marina cringed inwardly at the thought of being tucked against his chest, bleeding out and *dying,* her skin against his to soothe the dark magic festering inside him. Goddess, how embarrassing for her to have to be cradled like a small child. And by *Rom,* no less.

She would rather die. But, of course, dying was never an option for her.

"Fine," Marina grumbled. "But do we even know where we're going? I thought Rom had to cast a spell."

"That chimera came from the north," he said. "But just to be sure..." He lifted one hand and summoned a single black flame that encompassed each of his fingers. The silver of his eyes burned bright in the moonlight as he studied the flame. He closed his eyes, inhaling deeply, then doused the flame and dropped his hand. "North. Toward the mountains."

"Very well," said Farah. "North we go. Here, Marina." She shoved a bundle of rags into her hands. "Keep that pressed against the wound as tightly as you can to stop the bleeding. I know you're immortal, but it would spare you—and us—a lot of agony if your body *didn't* completely bleed out." She offered a grim smile as Marina accepted the rags, stifling a cry of pain as she pressed them against the slashes along her side.

Without warning, Rom scooped her up, one arm under her legs and the other behind her back. Her free hand flew out, pressing against his muscular chest in her desperation not to fall.

Rom smirked down at her. "I won't drop you. Promise."

"Forgive me if I don't take your word for it," Marina muttered, trying to get comfortable without nuzzling directly against his torso. He smelled like pine and woodsmoke and a musky manly scent that was so stark and familiar that for a brief moment, she was transported back to that night in the temple when he had pinned her against the wall and—

No. Marina shut out those thoughts immediately. She did not need reminders of that night, not when his body was so close to hers. Instead, she needed to remind herself that his very presence was the reason she was cursed. He had been careless enough to take a tumble with her without disclosing his identity, without *warning* her. And then, he'd vanished.

It didn't matter that it hadn't been his fault. It didn't matter that there was a perfectly valid reason for his continued absence—because Tethys had cursed him, too.

No, what *did* matter was that Marina had been foolish and careless, too. She had let his handsome looks and coy smile charm her, blurring all sense of logic and reason, lowering her inhibitions.

He was dangerous... because he was so desirable to her.

And she would never let herself fall for that again.

Biting her lip hard enough to taste blood, Marina closed her eyes as they set off, the jostling motion of being in Rom's arms achingly reminding her of a familiar river that flowed in the forest she grew up in—a river that would never flow again.

CHAPTER NINE

Marina slipped in and out of consciousness. One moment, she was overcome with fever dreams of pain and fire and three-headed demons. The next, she was shivering against Rom's chest as dust and sand swirled around her. Rom's pace was brisk, his strenuous breathing indicating how fast they were traveling. Silence and a crippling sense of urgency lingered among the witches. Marina tried to lift her head to see what was happening, to see if something was chasing them. But as she shifted, Rom grunted something and clutched her tighter against his chest.

She was too dazed to resist. Her eyes fluttered shut, and she fell asleep.

When she woke again, the air was colder, and something wet splashed along her face. Blinking, she gazed upward and found dark rain clouds filling the sky, heavy droplets falling on them as they traveled. Rom had a cloak pulled over his head, though Marina didn't remember them stopping to purchase supplies. He tried to shield her from the rainfall, but Marina pushed on his chest.

"Don't worry about me," she croaked. "Just keep going."

Rom said nothing, the only indication that the strain of carrying her and keeping such a brisk pace was wearing on him. How long had they been traveling? When had they last stopped?

"Keep applying pressure," said a steady voice. Warm hands pressed against her abdomen, and Marina cried out in agony. "You've lost too much blood."

Those same hands grabbed her fingers, placing them over the bloody cloth to hold it in place. But Marina was too weak. She couldn't put the necessary weight on it to keep it in place.

When she woke again, her skin was on fire. At first, she thought her fire magic was burning her up again. But this was different. Her flesh was scorching, sweat pouring down her face and neck. Despite this, she still shivered in Rom's arms.

Fever. Her wounds were infected. Cursing under her breath, Marina shut her eyes against the pain wracking her body. She could endure this. She'd experienced death before. This was nothing.

Her eyes closed again.

"You can get through this," Rom said. "You are strong, Mare."

Mare. The shortened name triggered something deep within her. An aching loss, a festering pain that lingered with her every day.

I love you, Mare. I always will.

Anguish mingled with her pain, reminding her of the mother she'd lost. The only other person to call her Mare.

Had Rom known this? Had he known the name would summon those memories and keep her conscious?

"We're almost there," Rom went on, his voice raspy. "Just a bit longer and we can get you the care you need. They've been chasing us for miles. It isn't safe just yet. But not much longer, I promise."

Marina was only partially paying attention. Her eyelids fluttered, her body longing for unconsciousness once more, but something told her this time was different. She was hot and cold all at once, her body numb from pain and dizzying disorientation.

The infection was killing her.

But wouldn't that be better? Why wouldn't Rom just let her give in and then they could revive her later?

No one wants to see you die, Marina. The thought was so stark in her mind that it surprised her. It was easy to retreat so far within herself that she didn't see anyone else, didn't care about anything but herself and her quest for revenge.

But things were different now. These witches cared for her. And Marina cared for them. Somehow, that certainty had taken root inside her, altering her awareness of herself and the life around her.

She wasn't alone anymore.

"Farah and Dahlia circled back to take out a couple of harpies that were stalking us," Rom said. "They should be back soon."

Dahlia. Marina remembered the midnight conversation she'd shared with the witch, and the affection she'd shown her. Several other witches had been kind to her, too, but Marina didn't know all of their names. How could she claim to care for them when she wouldn't even allow herself to get closer? To understand them better?

She'd trained herself too well to keep her distance. But it was safer this way. Safer for others, but also for herself. If *she* didn't care about anyone, then she wouldn't suffer when those around her inevitably perished. Not just from the curse, but from time. Marina would outlive them all. She would watch them wither and die.

And nothing could stop it. One way or another, everyone around her would die.

"We're almost to the Voiceless Jungle," Rom continued. Marina knew he was speaking for her benefit, to keep her lucid. "Have you been there before?"

An indistinguishable noise rose up Marina's throat. She had, in fact. There was something eerie and spooky about the jungle with no sound. No animals lived within it, only lush foliage that seemed to have a mind of its own. Legend told of a coven of earth witches that kept the plants alive, feeding their magic into the roots and the earth to keep out intruders. Not many ventured into the jungle.

Which was why Marina liked it so much. It was one of the few places where she could truly be alone. As long as she didn't disturb the earth witches, of course.

"There's so much of this realm I have yet to see," Rom said. "I've only watched from afar."

Marina felt her brow furrow with brief confusion, but she was too weak to speak. All she could do was hope Rom would continue rambling and answer her unasked questions.

"There is an ancient relic in the Underworld," he said. "A reflection bowl with the power to show you other realms. Other places. Other... people." His voice caught on that last word, only piquing Marina's interest. "My first and only visit to the Realm of Gaia was much shorter than I would have liked. After... after that night with you, I was pulled back against my will to face the wrath of Tethys, and the wrath of my father. And then the curse prevented me from ever coming back, though I certainly tried." He huffed a bitter laugh. "But this reflection bowl allowed me to look into this realm, to view the places I yearned to see. The Thanassian Empire. The Emdale Mountains. The Manos Ocean. So much life and beauty here that I don't have access to in my world." He paused, and Marina held her breath as she waited for him to go on. "And you."

Marina's heart lurched in her throat. She was fully awake now, though her face was pressed against Rom's shirt, and she didn't dare move in case she startled him into silence. She kept her eyes closed, but she yearned to look up at him and scrutinize his expression. Was he full of regret? Anger? Sorrow? What tragedies had he faced in the Underworld to make him so tormented? Was it Tartarus, or his brothers?

For the first time since she was cursed, Marina felt an aching desperation to know another person's mind, thoughts, and heart. She wanted to peel back every layer of Rom and understand who he was, where he came from, and what *his* life had been like since his own curse. So often she pushed away other people's trauma and pain, claiming her own was worse, that her life was so miserable that no one could possibly understand.

But every struggle was different. And here was someone who, quite possibly, had experienced horrors far worse than hers. Instead of shoving aside his pain, Marina found herself wanting to sift through it, to understand it, to *heal* it.

She had never felt anything like this before. Perhaps it was her raging fever.

Or perhaps it was the undeniable connection she felt to Rom and these witches. Against her will, their presence had opened her up.

"I used the reflection bowl to watch over you, Marina," Rom said, his voice strained, but she knew it wasn't from physical exertion. "I wanted... I wanted to make sure you were safe. And when I realized you *weren't*, I couldn't stop looking for you, hoping and praying and *pleading* that your life would improve, that you would find peace and happiness. I couldn't stop until I knew that much." He sniffed, and more liquid splashed along Marina's face—his tears. "It was my fault. All my fault. I —I was so careless and clueless and secretive. If I had been open with you from the beginning about who I was, none of this would have happened to you. I know my apologies will never be enough for the sorrows you've endured, but I wish you could know... wish you could understand the grief I feel for causing you so much pain. Every time I visited that reflection bowl, I yearned with every fiber of my being to find you safe and taken care of. Loved, even." He broke off with a shuddering breath. "But it never happened. And there was nothing I could do."

Marina's throat was so tight with emotion she could hardly breathe. Tears pooled in her own eyes, and she was grateful for the rainy weather to mask the droplets of her tears on his shirt. Goddess, she hadn't realized... hadn't *known*... All this time, Rom had been looking after her. He'd *remembered* her.

She'd spent years envisioning him living a carefree life among the other gods, laughing at her expense, forgetting her entirely.

But he had suffered. And he had remembered.

Just like her.

"I will do everything in my power to break your curse, Marina," Rom said in a low voice. "I swear it on my life, on my god's blood, on the very death magic that courses through my veins. I will not rest until you are freed."

But what about you? Marina wanted to ask. *Don't you deserve freedom, too?* She wanted to cling to him, to shake him, to shout that *his* curse was unfair and unjust, that Tethys had deprived them both of peace and happiness.

This wasn't Rom's fault. Or Marina's. It was Tethys's.

Rom's body shifted, and the sound of low, murmuring voices reached Marina's ears. She strained to hear what was being said, but it was drowned out by the rainfall around them. Then, she heard Farah's voice.

"All clear. The inn is up ahead, and I've already sent for a healer."

Thank the Goddess Farah was all right. Marina let herself relax against Rom's chest, the momentary clarity fading from her mind as she succumbed to her fever.

CHAPTER TEN

"Marina."

Marina shifted with a groan, her brain foggy and incoherent.

"*Marina.*"

Her eyes fluttered open, but a blurry haze obscured her vision. Why couldn't she see properly? She tried to move, but her body was stuck, completely frozen. Her lips parted, her mouth and throat dry as parchment. Her tongue was glued to the roof of her mouth.

Goddess, what was wrong with her?

"That's it. Keep pushing."

Marina tried to shake her head, to convey that she didn't understand. Keep pushing? What did that mean?

"Come back to us, Mare."

That name. That *voice*. She sucked in a sharp breath,

then immediately coughed as she choked on a nasty paste that was lodged in her throat. Her coughing intensified, and a glass of water was shoved into her hands. Marina blindly brought it to her mouth, gulping it down greedily.

"Easy. Not too much."

Though Marina wanted to keep chugging the soothing cool water that washed out the foul taste in her mouth, she reluctantly set the glass down and wiped her face. She blinked rapidly, clearing her vision and making out Rom's concerned face in front of her. She was lying on a lumpy bed in a small room with dusty furniture and old, moth-eaten drapes drawn in front of the window. Her eyes roved over the space, and she frowned when she realized she and Rom were alone.

"Farah," Marina said, sitting up quickly. "Wren. The others... where are they?"

"It's all right." Rom placed a hand on her shoulder, guiding her back to a reclined position. "They're safe. They needed to shift to their serpent forms and release some of their pent-up magic, but they'll be back soon."

Marina nodded, though her heart wouldn't stop racing. "How—How long?" She didn't need to clarify what she was asking.

Rom's face tightened. "You were sick with a fever for five days. We finally found a healer to tend to you, but it took three more days after that for you to finally come to.

Farah—Farah thinks an ordinary mortal would have perished already from the infection."

Marina's blood ran cold. *I would have died.* She glanced down at her shirt—which was different from the one she'd been wearing last—and rolled up the edges to inspect the bandages wrapped around her. The slashes still ached and throbbed, but it was dull and faint compared to before. She had a feeling if she peeled back the bandages, she would find nothing more than a few reddened marks that had almost entirely scabbed over.

"Eight days," she whispered. "Goddess, that's a long time." She stared at him. "What about your curse? Did you have any fits while I was unconscious?"

Rom shifted his weight from one foot to the other. "Yes. Farah told me to stay close to you, in case your presence alone would be enough."

When he said nothing, Marina raised her eyebrows. "And was it?" She wasn't sure why she cared, but her heart thundered loudly in her chest as she awaited his response.

"Yes and no. Twice I was able to clutch your hand in mine and ward off my death magic. Farah suspects the heat of your fever triggered a small bit of fire magic. For the third fit, I... had to endure until it ended."

Marina's eyes widened. "What? You could have died!"

Rom offered a wry smile. "Is that concern for me I detect?"

Marina snorted. "Hardly." But her nonchalance was forced, and they both knew it.

"Farah used her fire magic on me. It wasn't as powerful as yours, but it helped."

Marina frowned at this. Farah's magic wasn't as powerful as her own? That didn't seem right; Farah was twice the fire witch she was.

She changed the subject. "Where are we?"

"We crossed the Voiceless Jungle, and we're in the Thanassian Empire now," Rom told her. "We're staying at an inn as far from the castle as possible to avoid detection." He shot an apologetic look her way. "Sorry. The accommodations aren't the best. But it's inconspicuous."

Marina waved a hand. "I've seen far worse. This doesn't bother me." She paused, hesitating, as a flood of memories washed over her. Rom's confessions. The things he'd told her.

Did he know she'd been listening? Surely not. Surely, he wouldn't have exposed so much of himself to her. The thought made her cheeks grow hot, and she turned away, unable to look him in the eye.

"Any trouble along the way?" she asked, fiddling with a loose thread on the bedsheet.

"Nothing we couldn't handle. Though no one is quite as fierce as you are when it comes to battling demons." A smile spread across his face that sent warmth through Marina's chest.

"And the kelpies?" She forced her fluttering emotions down so she could focus on more important things.

Rom's face immediately sobered. "I've cast the spell often to ensure we're on the right track. They are hiding in the Emdale Mountains, near the coast. It'll be several days before we get there, but with you healed, it shouldn't be too difficult."

Guilt swelled inside her, and she shut her eyes, covering her face with her hands. "Goddess, I'm such a fool. If I hadn't been injured—If I—"

"Hey. Stop." Rom pressed his hand against hers, his silver eyes burning with intensity. "You defeated that chimera. You were *incredible*, Marina. It's a miracle you survived the attack at all. No one blames you for what happened."

Marina could only shake her head, dismissing his praise. It felt undeserved. Unwarranted. She'd been careless, taking advantage of her immortality. She often had to remind herself that living forever didn't mean she was invincible. It didn't make her immune to pain and injury.

And she'd slowed down their travels. What if the other witches died because of it? What horrors were the kelpies subjecting them to?

"How's Wren?" Marina asked, trying to disguise the tremor in her voice. "Any improvement?"

"Some. Every time a creature attacks, she relapses. But, thanks to you, the witches now know that a burst of their fire magic can bring her back." His eyes flared with anguish, and Marina knew it was a lot worse than he was implying. Yes, they could bring Wren back... but only temporarily.

She was still dying. And the presence of these demonic creatures was accelerating her fate.

Marina lay her head back on the pillow, momentarily wishing she could fall back into unconsciousness. Because the pain of reality was almost too much to bear.

Rom leaned forward and took her hand. Her first thought was to jerk away from his touch, but his skin was smooth against hers, and something about the contact soothed the roiling emotions inside her.

"It isn't your fault," Rom said.

"I know," Marina said at once. "It's just... being around other people again... *caring* for them again..." She bit her lip. "It's harder than I remembered. I—I *can't* lose anyone else, Rom. I can't."

He nodded gravely, his thumb tracing circles around her knuckles, the sensation sending prickles of energy and awareness throughout her body. Marina thought of all he'd confessed to her—of his desperation to find her happy and safe.

She leaned forward, clasping his hand tightly in hers. "Rom—"

She faltered when she noticed the inky markings winding around his arm. Brow furrowed, she sat up straighter, bringing his arm closer so she could inspect it. It looked just like the coils of darkness that surrounded him when his curse had tried to take him.

"Rom, what is this?" she asked sharply.

He withdrew his hand, his expression guarded. But Marina was determined to find the truth. As fiercely as she could manage, she said, "Tell me."

He groaned and ran a hand through his hair. "It's my curse. It leaves a mark every time it tries to pull me back."

"Every time?" Marina's heart fluttered in fear. "But... what happens when those markings are all over your body?"

Rom met her gaze with grim sorrow. Marina knew the answer from that expression alone.

Either the Underworld would succeed in pulling him back... or he would die.

"Can't—Can't Farah do something?" Marina asked.

He shook his head. "It's death magic. It's beyond her understanding. She thinks being around Pandora's magic so often is making it worse."

Marina shook her head, refusing to accept that this was *it*. That eventually his curse would win. "She promised she'd help you break the curse! There has to be *something*."

Rom averted his gaze, but not before some unknown emotion flared in his gaze.

"Rom," Marina said. "There's more, isn't there?"

Rom exhaled heavily. "Farah believes that you are the key to undoing my curse. And I'm the key to undoing yours. That... whatever tethers us together is the link to Tethys's magic. Together, we were cursed. And together, we can be cured."

Marina swallowed hard. *Together, we can be cured.* If her touch could heal him—even temporarily—it would make sense that some part of her was the key to his freedom. She thought about what Dahlia had said... that it was clear Rom and Marina were connected in this curse somehow.

But how could Marina discover the answers in time to save him? She'd been around him for days now, and his curse was still one step ahead, ready to claim him at a moment's notice. Was it some kind of spell? Was it connected to her fire magic?

"Farah knows all manner of ancient spells," Rom went on. "She thinks she can experiment with both our powers and find the answer."

"When?" Marina snapped. "In between battling Pandora's demons and keeping Wren alive? Before or after we reach the kelpies and rescue the other witches?

That's assuming the kelpies don't kill us all first—or your curse takes you before then." A hot lump of anger and regret rose up her throat. She tried to swallow it down, but it only burned more, igniting within her.

She couldn't do this. She couldn't. This was why she kept pushing Rom away. She was drawn to him, connected to him in ways she couldn't explain or prevent. But she never wanted to let him into her heart again. She told herself if she despised him, if she could blame *him* for her curse, then she would be safe.

But she'd failed. She couldn't loathe him. Not as much as she wanted to.

Rom leaned forward, taking both her hands in his. Marina's eyes were immediately drawn to the inked markings crawling up his arm, and she suppressed a shudder.

"Mare," Rom said, his voice barely above a whisper. "I'm still here. It hasn't taken me yet. And when it tries to, I swear I'll put up a hell of a fight. We are in this together. We can fight this *together*. I believe it."

Marina wanted to believe it, too. But she'd seen so much tragedy and despair in her life that it was hard to cling to that hope.

Hope was dangerous. Hope could destroy her. In many ways, it already had.

She met his silvery gaze, and his eyes shone with such fierceness and determination that she felt some of her anguish crumble. There was so much power and fury in his expression that, for a moment, she thought she recognized her own fire. Her own blazing inferno.

Rom had his own kind of flame. While Marina's burned amber and furious, Rom's was cool and silvery blue. Calm and controlled, but just as deadly, if not more so than Marina's. The sight of it made her breath catch, and she felt drawn in, pulled closer by the sheer force of his power.

Here was magic that could destroy worlds, level cities, re-create the entire realm. But Rom kept it so contained, so caged, that he never let anyone see it.

Until now.

Marina was the same. She kept herself sealed off from the world, hiding her true nature, her true self.

She leaned closer to him, ready to dive into the depths of his power, ready to free herself, to free *him*—

A sharp, piercing sensation pulsed in her chest, and Marina pressed a hand to her breast, crying out in pain. She sucked in sharp gasps, and an icy coldness sliced through her, freezing her fire and numbing her bones.

It felt as if the fire within her had been doused by a wave of ice-cold water.

She was on her feet in a flash, her body swaying and her head spinning. Rom's hands grasped her shoulders, his eyes full of alarm.

"Marina, what—"

"Something is wrong," Marina said, still rubbing her chest. The strange feeling wouldn't abate, but she *knew* that feeling. It felt like a distant memory. Like a home she once had.

The magic of rivers. *Water* magic.

"Take me to the other witches," she told Rom. "*Now.*"

CHAPTER ELEVEN

To his credit, Rom didn't argue with her. Either he could sense the magic, too, or he understood from Marina's urgency that there was no use in arguing.

A water mage was nearby. A *powerful* one.

The coven wasn't safe.

Rom looped his arm through Marina's and guided her out the dank room and down the stairs before they hurried out the back door. A chilled breeze swept over them when they stepped outside, a stark contrast to the dry and hot desert air Marina had grown accustomed to.

"There's a small copse of trees down the road," Rom said, pointing past several squat houses. "That's where they shifted."

The icy pulse of power resonated in Marina's chest, burning just as intensely as her own flames. It was the kind of cold that felt like fire, numbing and consuming every part of her. She shivered, and Rom's grip on her arm tightened. She wanted to break into a run, but her body was still recovering. All she could manage was a brisk stride, but it didn't feel fast enough.

"Do you feel it?" Marina asked, her teeth chattering.

"I didn't before," Rom said. "But I do now. Someone powerful is here." His gaze cut to hers, and they exchanged a solemn look.

It seemed to take an eternity before they finally reached the small grove of trees. Marina stepped into the shaded canopy without preamble, trying to summon her fire magic to sense the serpents nearby. But the ice magic was too strong, too potent for her to get past.

Could she even conjure her own magic if it came to a fight?

And *why* was she so helpless? She'd been around water mages before and had never been rendered this powerless.

"Where are they?" Marina whispered to Rom, her voice carrying in the eerily silent wood. It was as startling as the Voiceless Jungle. No animals. No insects. Not a twig snapped; not a leaf fell.

It was as still as death itself.

Rom conjured black flames in his free hand, his face a hard mask of fury. "A god is here."

Marina's heart lurched. *A god?* Dread pooled in her stomach.

A god... with water magic... That meant—

"Ah, there she is," crooned a horribly familiar voice. A voice that haunted Marina's dreams every night.

Marina's body went stiff, as if the goddess's magic had frozen her completely. A glowing figure appeared, her aura casting a light within the dark forest. Her springy curls were pulled into a loose knot on one side of her neck, and she wore the same aquamarine tiara as the last time Marina had seen her. Unlike the loose white dress, she wore gleaming gold armor and wielded a long, magnificent sword in one hand.

Tethys. And she was here for battle.

"It's been quite a long time, dear, hasn't it?" Tethys offered a sickly sweet smile.

"What are you doing here?" Marina found her voice at last and was grateful it didn't quiver. She balled her hands into fists, allowing her rage to consume her, to melt away the ice that had frozen her insides.

"Did you really think you and your filthy witches could roam these lands without my knowing?" Tethys chuckled as she drew closer. "The kelpies belong to me, and I won't let you hurt them. Your precious Hestia can't possibly protect *all* of you."

Before Marina could react, Tethys summoned a long, sharpened icicle in her free hand and hurled it toward her. Marina's hands shot up in defense, but Rom's black flame intercepted the icicle, melting it before it reached her. To Marina's surprise, twin flames appeared in her hands, ready to defend her. The sight spurred her onward, and she called on the full force of her fire magic.

Consume, she commanded it. *Be free.*

She could've sworn she heard another presence inside her, someone who sighed with relief and gratitude, before her entire body erupted in flames. To her immense satisfaction, Tethys staggered back a step, her eyes wide with alarm.

"Where are the others?" Marina roared, her voice a booming, echoing sound in the forest.

Tethys recovered quickly, a snarl twisting her face as she gripped her sword in both hands. "You're too late, you Gorgon hag. The fire witches are *mine.* And your power is no match for the destruction I wield."

She charged, but Marina was ready. By the time Tethys had reached her, Marina had shifted to her serpent form, mouth open wide and fangs flashing. A blast of Rom's black magic appeared between them, spearing Tethys directly in the face and momentarily blinding her. Tethys shrieked, and Marina took advantage, sinking her fangs into the goddess's throat.

Tethys was undeterred. She struck with her sword, even as Marina's assault sent her sprawling to the forest floor. The blade connected with Marina's scales, and blood burst from the injury. She hissed in pain, but wound around Tethys, avoiding another strike as they tumbled to the ground together. Marina twisted around Tethys's throat, tightening and tightening. Then Rom was there, sending another blast of his deadly magic, keeping Tethys's hands busy so she couldn't slash at Marina again.

"You—cannot—kill—me!" Tethys rasped as Marina continued to strangle her.

But Marina didn't care. She would do as much damage as she could to this vile goddess, the reason behind her suffering. Behind Rom's suffering.

Rom pressed a hand against the goddess's chest, his face blazing with fury. "Marina might not have the magic of the gods," he growled, "but I do. Tell us where the other witches are, or I swear on my god's blood I will end your existence right here and now without a drop of remorse."

Uncertainty flared in Tethys's eyes. "You're lying," she spat. "I am under Neptune's protection. You cannot hurt me without incurring his mighty wrath."

"The Underworld is gone," Rom said, baring his teeth at her. "I have nothing left. Let the wrath of your precious sea god consume me—let all of Elysium consume me. I don't care. If it means ending your pitiful life, I'll do it."

True fear crept into Tethys's gaze. Marina coiled tighter around her throat, pleased to find the goddess's skin turning a sickly blue.

"Last chance," Rom warned. Black spirals of flame coated his hand, melting away the armor on Tethys's chest.

"All right!" Tethys cried. "Release me, and I'll—I'll tell you."

Rom withdrew his hand, but Marina wasn't as trusting. She only loosened her hold a fraction, keeping her body wound around the goddess. Tethys sat up, snarling at both of them. "I trapped them in a water vice about a mile from here. They are alive, but weakened."

Marina hissed in anger. *Weakened?* As if these witches hadn't suffered enough...

She slowly extracted her body from Tethys's. As soon as she did, the goddess moved so swiftly, Marina didn't even see the blow coming. Her sword slashed, but not at Marina—at Rom. The blade buried in his shoulder, and he cried out, falling to his knees.

Marina surged forward, trying to coil around Tethys once more, but a wall of water appeared between them, cutting off Marina's access. Tethys raised her sword again, lunging for Rom—

Marina screamed, and a burst of fire burned through the water magic, evaporating it completely. Steam filled the air, and Marina, her serpent form encompassed in flames, darted toward the goddess. Her fangs pierced the soft flesh of her ankles, then the sparse part of her kneecap not covered in armor.

Tethys fell to one knee, crying out. Marina bit again and again, her fangs sinking into every piece of exposed flesh she could find.

With a scream, Tethys swiped her sword over and over, blindly stabbing at Marina. She felt the sharpened point pierce her scales once, twice, three times... but Marina continued her assault, undeterred. She would end this goddess, even if it killed her...

A massive explosion of fire lit up the forest, and for a moment, Marina thought her magic had become so out of control that she had set the entire wood on fire. But within those flames formed a figure, her wild hair billowing in the wind. As the fire faded, Marina found herself staring openly at the woman standing before them. She had fiery red hair and identical crimson eyes that flashed with intensity and rage. A shimmering gold gown hung over one shoulder, accentuating the muscles in her arms. She may not have been dressed for battle, but she was a warrior all the same.

And though Marina had never met her before, she knew exactly who she was: Hestia.

CHAPTER TWELVE

MARINA COULD DO NOTHING BUT STARE AT THE majestic goddess standing before her. She didn't even register that she had shifted back to human form and was sitting—naked and covered in blood—on the forest floor. Her magic was spent. Every inch of her body was throbbing in pain, her flesh on fire from the intensity of the magic she'd expended and the wounds Tethys had inflicted.

Tethys unleashed a feral screech and lunged for Hestia, raising her sword. Hestia lifted one palm, and flames encircled the water goddess, blocking her path.

"Is this really where you choose to make your last stand, Tethys?" Hestia said coldly. "You are outnumbered. Go. Lick your wounds."

"I do not take orders from *you*," Tethys spat, still

wielding her sword. But even Marina could tell the goddess was weak. Silver blood streamed down her face and neck, and her eyes were slightly bloodshot. "I serve the mighty Neptune, and his power could obliterate you in seconds."

Hestia lifted her chin. "Yes, but is Neptune here? To me, it seems you are the only threat. Between me, my vessel, and this death god, we outnumber you. If this is your choice, I will not hold back. I will see to your destruction on this day. But right now, I offer you mercy. Take it, and leave this place."

The intensity in Tethys's face faltered as she glanced from Marina to Hestia to Rom, who was still on his knees, clutching at the bleeding wound on his shoulder.

"Your fight is with me," Hestia said. "Not them."

"They fight for *you*," Tethys snarled. "If they are not with me, they are against me. They are against Neptune himself."

"*Leave*, Tethys." Lightning flashed in the sky, and Hestia's eyes burned with scorching fury.

Tethys staggered back a step, and the flames surrounding her vanished. "I swear to the gods of Elysium, you will pay for this. If not by my hand, then by the hand of the sea god himself." With those ominous words, Tethys disappeared in a plume of white smoke. Water droplets sprayed in the air with her departure.

"What have you done?" Marina cried, trying to rise,

but the gaping wounds in her side and arms dragged her back down. Lightheaded, she sank to the ground, her body numb from blood loss. "We could have finished her!"

"We could have done no such thing," Hestia said sharply. "I was bluffing."

Brief confusion crept into Marina's muddled thoughts. "Bluffing?"

"I don't have the power to end her. I never did."

Cold dread filled Marina's veins. No. It couldn't be true. If Hestia couldn't defeat Tethys, then who could?

"And you still have far to go before you can access your full power," Hestia went on, as if she hadn't just delivered earth-shattering news to Marina.

"She will only keep hunting my kind," Marina said. "She has to be stopped!"

"You are right." Hestia fixed her brilliant red eyes on Marina. "But during our great war, while Tethys used the dark and forbidden magic of Pandora, I used the power of the titans, who are now imprisoned. The source of my power is inaccessible. Tethys doesn't know this, but it won't take long before she discovers she can overpower me. When she does, she will decimate me and my followers. And with Neptune on her side, she will be unstoppable."

Marina thought of the coven of fire witches who had

taken her in and protected her. They would be slaughtered by Tethys and her dark creatures.

"What can we do?" Rom asked. His face was deathly pale, but his eyes were full of fire.

"You must seek out your sisters, Marina," Hestia said. "Only together can you unleash the power of the Gorgons."

Marina shook her head. "I'm already with the fire witches."

"Not the fire witches. There are three Gorgon sisters. You have the soul of one. You must find the other two and unite your magic before your powers can be harnessed."

Marina shook her head, her muddied thoughts struggling to keep up. "I don't understand. With my curse—"

"Tethys only cursed you with the powers you already have. She's using your magic against you. You are the key to unlocking your curse. And his." Her gaze cut to Rom's. "The Gorgon blood running through your veins has the ability to break powerful curses. You only need to learn how to use it."

Marina gritted her teeth, dizzy from the pain threatening to consume her. "*What* power? What magic? You say I only need to learn how to use it, but *how* can I learn? If I have all this power, how the hell can I use it?"

"Only you know the answer to that. Only you can

discover it for yourself." Hestia cocked her head slightly, her shrewd eyes narrowing. "You are dying."

"I'm immortal," Marina snapped. "I'll be fine."

Hestia shook her head. "You've been dealt a death blow from an immortal blade. This is no ordinary injury, Marina. It will claim you until you can be healed properly. I may not be able to slay our enemies, but I *can* heal you from Tethys's attack."

Hestia approached, but Marina shrank away from her. As much as she yearned to be healed, to end the agony burning in her veins, she couldn't shake the thought of the fire witches from her mind.

"Free them first," Marina said. "I don't want to be healed while they are still imprisoned."

Hestia's brow furrowed. "I cannot help those imprisoned by the kelpies. My power only extends so far. But those whom Tethys has trapped, I can certainly free."

"And Wren," Marina went on, unable to stop herself. "Heal her, too. Please."

Hestia's eyes gleamed. "You care for them."

"They're my sisters," Marina said without thought. "My kin. They have Gorgon blood, too."

Hestia nodded solemnly. "This is true. They may not be a direct vessel like you, but they are my followers. I will free them and heal them for you, Marina... if you swear to me you will exert every effort in unlocking your abilities. I have gifted you my power, but that comes at a price. You must fight for me. You must become my soldier. My blade."

Hestia's soldier. As foggy as her mind was, Marina couldn't contain the ripple of shock that swept over her. "I don't understand. How did I become your vessel? Why me?" She thought of Farah, so strong and capable. Surely, she would have been a better option.

"The soul of your serpent called to the Gorgons," Hestia said, as if this answer explained everything. "The soul of Medusa chose you."

Medusa. The name brought prickles of awareness along Marina's arms, strong enough to overcome her injuries for a brief moment. She'd been told stories of the Gorgon priestess, defiled by Neptune and cursed with the power to turn men to stone. Some called her a monster for it. Others revered her as a goddess.

Marina had never given much thought to Medusa's tale... until now.

Of course there was a link between herself and Medusa. How had she not seen it before? Marina, too, had been cursed by a water deity—cursed to turn others into stone.

She couldn't possibly deny Hestia's claim. The evidence was so striking that Marina felt it in her core: she *was* connected to Medusa's spirit.

Hestia drew closer and placed a palm against Marina's forehead. Marina was too stunned and consumed with agony to move away from her touch. As the goddess's burning flesh met Marina's skin, a sharp, intense wave of heat washed over her. She gasped, but Hestia kept her palm firmly against her, holding her in place.

"The fire is not just a part of you, my child," Hestia said. "The fire *is* you."

Her words resonated down to Marina's bones, making her whole body quiver.

"What is your answer?" Hestia asked. "Will you swear yourself to me as my soldier and my blade?"

Marina blinked as a dark fog crept into her vision. She would faint from blood loss soon. Her time was limited. "I will." The words poured readily from her lips, and the truth of her conviction startled her. She *would* give anything, pay any price, to keep her friends alive. She had seen so much death, caused so much loss... She couldn't bear any more of it.

If she had to fight in Hestia's name, then so be it.

Hestia inclined her head. "Then, our bargain is struck."

Hestia's magic incinerated Marina from the inside out. In a flash of amber and gold, she succumbed to unconsciousness, letting Hestia's flames consume her.

CHAPTER THIRTEEN

Marina's dreams were plagued by smoke and ash, the vacant stares of those turned to stone at her hand. Fangs and torment and anguish...

But this time, it was different. This time, she was a creature of her own making, something to be feared, to cause destruction. Her form changed, and she became part serpent, part flame. Her hair turned into coils of snakes, her eyes flashing gold that rendered her enemies powerless with a single look.

She unleashed an almighty roar of triumph, bursting into battle as she slaughtered foe after foe. She had never felt so powerful before. Gone were her insecurities and regrets. Gone was her thirst for revenge.

This, here and now, was her victory. And hers alone.

Marina jolted awake, her skin still burning as if the

flames still coated her body. She touched the frayed ends of her hair, half expecting it to be serpents. Her heart thundered loudly inside her chest, and it took her a moment to ground herself and remember what had happened.

Hestia. Tethys.

Medusa.

Suppressing a shudder, Marina sat up, swinging her legs over the cot she'd fallen asleep on. The room was unfamiliar to her, indicating someone had carried her here. Rom, perhaps? No one else had been around. The idea of being in his arms, cradled against his muscular chest, made her throat go dry. The room was sparsely furnished, with only a small desk on the opposite side and a faded gray carpet on the dusty floorboards.

Marina lurched to her feet, remembering the other fire witches. Had Hestia freed them? Had she healed Wren? Where were they?

She was halfway to the door when she faltered, glancing down at her body with a soft gasp. Her injuries —the gashes, the blood—were gone. She lifted her arms, marveling at the stretch of pale skin, unmarred by wounds. Not even a scar remained from her fight with Tethys. Even the faded scars from the fight with the chimera had vanished.

Hestia had kept her word. Which meant the fire witches had to be safe.

But Marina needed to know for sure.

She bolted out the door and found herself in a narrow hallway lined with doors identical to hers. Another inn, it seemed. It didn't take her long to find the staircase. As she descended, she gazed below at the tavern underneath, finding a nearly empty room with a few patrons enjoying a drink. Sunlight filtered in through the windows, and Marina estimated it was early afternoon, which explained the absence of a crowd.

Among those in the tavern was one face she recognized: Rom. Logically, this made sense; Farah had said only Marina and Rom could properly blend in, so the rest of the fire witches were likely hiding somewhere, undetected. But that didn't stop Marina's stomach from flipping at the sight of his wavy black hair streaked with silver, the way his otherworldly eyes darted around the room, no doubt searching for threats. He hadn't seen her descending the staircase yet, so Marina allowed herself another moment to study him undisturbed. His arm was still marked with ink, a sign of his realm trying to reclaim him. His facial hair had grown a bit more, looking slightly unkempt, but not in an unpleasant way. If anything, it made him look more rugged. Less tame. The thought sent a bolt of heat and desire through Marina's belly, reminding her of their night together. How unrestrained they'd both been.

As if sensing the direction of her thoughts, Rom's

eyes cut to hers, his silver eyes flashing. She froze at the foot of the stairs, holding his gaze. Something flared between them, something she couldn't name. Rom rose to his feet, his eyes still pinned to hers as he made his way to her. The closer he got, the more her skin warmed at his proximity, as if her body were heating in anticipation of his nearness. When he stood before her, his expression fierce and full of an intensity that made her tremble, she merely looked up at him, waiting for him to speak. She wasn't sure if she could; something about his powerful presence had rendered her speechless.

Or perhaps it was what they had faced together that had her frozen stiff. They were no longer enemies. She couldn't deny that any longer. They had fought together. They had saved each other's lives.

She wasn't sure what Rom was to her, but he was not her enemy.

"You saved my life," he murmured, his voice low and full of emotion.

Marina wasn't sure what she'd expected him to say first, but it wasn't this. This acknowledgment of what they were—and weren't—to each other. A question burned in his gaze: *why?* But Marina couldn't answer it. She didn't know why. It would've been so easy to let Tethys destroy him. How often had Marina sworn to do that exact thing if she ever encountered Rom again?

"You carried me halfway across the realm when I

was bleeding out," Marina said. "It was the least I could do."

Rom shook his head slightly. "Don't do that. Don't diminish your actions as if they meant nothing. Because mine didn't."

Marina's face flushed, and she couldn't hold his gaze any longer. She scanned the tavern once more. "Where are the others?"

"In Farah's room. They thought it best you recover in isolation. I was to wait for you when you emerged."

Marina frowned. "Isolation? Why?"

Rom blinked at her as if she'd grown a second head. "You are Hestia's chosen vessel. You aren't just an ordinary fire witch anymore, Marina. This changes everything."

Marina's stomach twisted at his words. She didn't want this. She didn't want the fire witches to look at her differently. All her life, she'd been different. An outcast. A monster, constantly being hunted. For the first time, she'd found a place to belong; a place where she wasn't feared or ridiculed or despised because of the magic flowing through her veins.

But now, because of what Hestia had said, all of that was gone. Her family. Her sense of belonging. The possibility that she could have created a home here.

No. Now, she was Hestia's vessel. Chosen by the Gorgons.

The soul of Medusa.

She felt Rom watching her, scrutinizing her. She fought to school her emotions and arrange her expression into something neutral, but the flare of empathy in his eyes indicated he'd already seen too much. He always could see more of her than she wanted him to.

But she didn't want his pity. Gritting her teeth, she lifted her chin and said, "Take me to them."

Rom nodded once, guiding her back up the stairs and down the hallway. Rom knocked lightly on a room a few doors down from hers, and a few seconds later, the door swung open.

Peering around Rom's bulky form, Marina made out a pentagram chalked on the floor, surrounded by candles. The smell of incense and fire magic filled the air, making Marina's head swim. The powerful energies in this room were enough to make her serpent rise within her, eager to be let loose.

Rom stepped inside, and Marina followed. She faltered when every single witch rose to her feet and bowed her head in silent reverence to her.

Marina lifted her hands, her chest tightening with discomfort and unease. "Please. Please don't."

"Hestia blessed," Farah murmured, pressing her hand to her heart. The witches next to her did the same.

"*Please.*" Marina felt on the verge of tears. "I don't want this. This isn't—This isn't me."

"We do not always choose our paths," Farah said. "Sometimes, they are chosen for us."

Marina drew closer to her. "I don't care who I am or what kind of magic flows through me. I am still the same person, the same witch you first met. Please don't treat me any differently. I'm not a goddess. I'm not a deity or a queen or anything. I know things have changed, but I'm still your equal. Your friend. Your sister." *I hope,* she wanted to add. Perhaps these witches never saw her as more than a dangerous stranger who had brought dark magic to their coven. But as she gazed at each of them, their eyes shone with respect and admiration. Some looked at her with awe, others with broad smiles.

Then, a figure emerged from the circle, flinging her arms around Marina in a tight embrace.

"Wren," Farah hissed in admonishment.

But Wren only clung to her tighter, and Marina returned the embrace, her eyes stinging with unshed tears.

"You saved us all," Wren whispered against her shoulder. "You saved *me.* I'll never forget this, Marina. You will always be my sister. Always."

Tears pooled in Marina's eyes and she couldn't stop them from streaming down her face. She withdrew to look Wren over and found her face full of color, the bandages gone from her head. The gash on her scalp was completely healed, the hair regrown as if the injury had never been there.

A lump formed in Marina's throat. "Goddess, Wren, I'm so glad you're healed." Her lower lip trembled, and more tears trickled down her cheeks.

"Because of *you*," Wren repeated. "You have no idea what you've done for me. For all of us."

Marina shook her head. "Hestia would've saved you anyway. You're her kin. Her people."

"No," Farah said. "Hestia broke the sacred laws of Elysium when she imbued our souls with the souls of serpents. She has been forbidden from interacting with us ever since. What she did for us was a great risk. I have no doubt the gods are raging at her for it right now."

Marina's jaw dropped. "She can't—She can't help you? Any of you? But you have a portal in those caves. I thought—"

"You thought we were close friends with the fire goddess?" Wren smirked. "Not quite. That portal was built for emergencies because of the goddess blood flowing through our veins. It was really just a formality. All those with goddess blood should have access to one." She shook her head. "No, we've been on our own for generations now."

Marina's head was swimming as she tried to process all of this. She looked at Farah, stunned to find the coven leader's face shining with pride.

"Hestia must really want you as her soldier," Farah whispered. "What an honor this is, Marina."

Marina was shaking her head again. "No. This has to be some kind of mistake."

Farah drew closer and took Marina's shoulders. "It is *not* a mistake. Tell me where you came from, Marina."

Marina's mouth opened and closed. She couldn't think. Couldn't even process a coherent thought.

"Marina. Where did you come from?"

"A—A coven of fire witches. I think. A water witch found me roaming the woods as a toddler and took me in, raising me as her own."

"And you never found your people?"

"She told me they were all killed. I sustained injuries, too. Whoever killed my coven must have assumed I'd died as well."

Farah smiled sadly and shook her head. "For hundreds of years, there have been tales of the three Gorgon sisters uniting once more and joining their powers. Two of them were rumored to be among us already. But it wasn't until twenty years ago that whispers of Medusa's heir spread through the fire witches. A prophecy foretold the birth of the Gorgon sister as Hestia's chosen vessel, marked with strength and power. Once she reunited with her sisters, they would combine their magic to end the war with the water gods. Even we heard the whispers, tucked away in the desert as we were.

"Tethys sent her witches across the realm, searching for this chosen vessel. Without Medusa, the sisters would be unable to reunite. The prophecy would be thwarted. The water witches hunted fire witches relentlessly, hoping that the more they killed, the less likely Medusa's vessel would emerge."

Marina's skin turned cold. "What—What are you saying?"

"I'm saying it was no coincidence a coven of river witches found you, Marina. They were sent to kill you."

CHAPTER FOURTEEN

Despite the earth-shattering revelation Farah had shared with her, Marina insisted they keep moving. Hestia had said she was unable to help the fire witches trapped by the kelpies, which meant they were in worse danger than they'd thought. And what Marina needed more than anything right now was a distraction. A purpose. A mission.

There were people who needed her help, and she couldn't let them down.

She tried to focus her thoughts on this task, the pursuit of her fellow fire witches. Not the devastating truth that the coven she'd grown up with—her family—had been sent to kill her. That Remy had lied to her all those years. That there was a reason the river witches had despised her so.

Her mind was a flurry of questions. How had Remy convinced the coven to accept her instead of kill her? Had she played on their sympathy, insisting it would be wrong to murder a child? Or had she convinced them there had been a mistake and Marina *wasn't* the chosen vessel of Medusa?

She supposed it didn't matter in the end. The entire coven was dead, including Remy. And Marina truly *was* Medusa's vessel. The Gorgon reincarnated.

A monster.

Marina tried not to notice how the other fire witches behaved around her. They either gave her a wide berth as they traveled, or they openly stared at her as if expecting her to morph into Medusa at any moment.

The only one whose behavior hadn't changed was Rom. She often caught him watching her, his gaze contemplative as always, but he said nothing. He remained close, and Marina noted how his hands curled into fists and the veins and tendons stood out along his arms and neck. He was fighting his curse actively. And it was happening more frequently.

They crossed the forest that skirted around the Thalassian Empire and made camp at the edge of the woods just outside the base of the Emdale Mountains. According to Rom's magic, the kelpies' nest was on the other side of the mountains.

They were so close. So close...

And yet, what manner of horrors were those witches enduring while Marina and the others were traveling? What if they got there too late?

My fault. All my fault. The thoughts kept circling through Marina's head.

The other fire witches shifted to their snake forms. Marina's inner serpent stirred slightly as she watched them, but her magic remained still. She wasn't sure if this was due to years of suppressing it, or if her magic was at peace and didn't need to be unleashed right now. She couldn't tell.

Her eyes fell on Rom, who sat on a log as he stared into the flames of their campfire, his gaze distant and full of anguish. After deliberating for a moment, Marina rose and joined him, sitting next to him on the log.

"Tell me about Tartarus," Marina said quietly.

Rom blinked, his expression strained. "What?"

"You accused me of not knowing your life, and you're right. I want to know what you've been through, Rom. Tell me."

Rom's eyes narrowed. "And why is that? To fuel your guilt over our curse? Or to distract you from what you're too afraid to face?"

Marina's head reared back. "What the hell are you talking about?"

"I refuse to feed your guilt, Marina. And I refuse to be a distraction for you. Whatever your reasons for this conversation are, it's for *your* sake and not mine. And I don't want any part of it."

Anger burned within her. "You don't know *anything*."

"Don't I? I was tasked with tormenting the most vile of souls down in Tartarus. And more often than not, a man's greatest fear was born of his own grief and guilt. Our demons are of our own making. The same applies to you. *You* are your greatest enemy, Marina. And I'm not going to play a part in this twisted game you're playing with yourself."

"This isn't a *game*," Marina seethed. "You think I *want* to feel this way? To hate myself and the monster that I am? You were right when you accused me of not bothering to know you, and now I'm trying to fix that. To look beyond myself, even though that defies what I've trained myself to do for fifty years. I'm not using you as a distraction or as a way to feed my guilt. I genuinely want to know."

"All right, fine." Rom shifted on the log, turning to face her fully. "Prove me wrong, Marina. Prove to me you aren't running from something. Before I tell you about my past, you tell me about yours. Tell me about the night you were cursed. What happened?"

Marina's throat closed as she stared at his hard expression. The emotions from that night swirled within her, threatening to choke her, to drown her. "I don't owe you an explanation," she said, her voice strained.

"Neither do I." Rom crossed his arms and raised his eyebrows. "But if you want to ask me questions, then I deserve the same. Trust goes both ways, Marina. I'm not going to open myself up to my past trauma just to provide you with a distraction. This isn't a game for me, either. So prove me wrong."

The air fell still around them, save for the crackling fire and the occasional hissing of one of the witches. Marina pressed her lips together to keep them from trembling. She wanted to argue, to rage at Rom and his insinuations... but he was right. She was using him as a diversion, something to preoccupy herself with so she wouldn't have to focus on her own emotions. And anything she learned about his past *would* fuel her guilt.

Because all of this was her fault. And she needed to remind herself she was a monster. It was the only thing keeping her from cursing her mother's name for hiding this monumental secret for so long.

And yet... Marina was alive because of Remy's choice. A mixture of anger and gratitude, sorrow and longing, filled Marina's chest so fully that her insides burned as if her fire magic had been kindled.

I've earned this pain and this suffering, Marina thought. *A monster like me should be hunted. Slaughtered. I deserve to be alone.*

But with Rom watching her, and that darkness creeping into his eyes, Marina had to remind herself it wasn't just about her. Yes, she understood Rom was a victim as well. Because of Tethys, he had been stranded, unable to leave the deepest, darkest part of the Underworld. But Marina had only scratched the surface of his pain and sorrow. Because she hadn't *wanted* to delve deeper. She hadn't wanted to learn more about his pain because she was so consumed by her own.

But things were different now. She was no longer alone.

With a deep, shuddering breath, Marina shifted on the log so she faced away from him, staring into the fire. She couldn't look into his eyes as she told him everything. For the first time in her life, Marina shared the darkest part of her past; the part she kept hidden and locked away for fear of letting it devour her entirely. As she spoke, the tears poured from her eyes, trailing down her cheeks. But she let them fall as she recounted the details of that day when she'd woken up and found her coven had turned to stone. When she'd realized the deadly consequences of her actions—and Tethys's wrath. That raw, festering pain came rushing back all at once, and she wanted to fall to her knees, to give in to it completely. But she forced herself to remain upright, to stay strong as she told her story. And as her voice grew hoarse and her tears dried up, exhaustion took over, and the pain dulled to an aching throb. It was still there, but it was weakened. Not nearly as potent as the day she'd lost her family.

It was bearable. For now.

Marina took another breath before she forced herself to meet Rom's gaze. His expression had softened, his eyes moist with his own tears. "When you told me you'd watched me through that reflection bowl, I realized I wasn't alone," she said. "*You* shared my grief, too, but I never knew. And I want to do the same for you, Rom. I want to share your burden, too. Just as you've shared mine."

Rom's face paled, his mouth going slack with shock. It was clear he hadn't realized she'd been listening to his confession when she'd been sick with the fever. She could only offer him a grimace as she waited for his response. After a moment, his expression cleared, and he nodded once.

"Tartarus messes with your mind," he said quietly. "It plays on your fears and emotions. Even if you tell yourself it's an illusion, it can still deceive you. All it needs is one moment of your doubt, and then it will snare you. It took years of practice with my own magic before I was comfortable enough to navigate those caves without getting sucked in. But the things I saw..." He shuddered and dropped his gaze. "The horrors I had to endure... I can never forget them. They haunt me, even now."

"What horrors?" Marina asked.

Rom offered her a pained expression. "I see that day. With you. I see you bleeding out on the stone floor. I see my brothers torturing you for sport, tearing apart your body piece by piece. I see dozens of other mortals like you, cursed because of me, slaughtered because of me. A world of death because of my one journey to the mortal realm."

Marina's chest felt hollow from this admission, but she forced herself to remain calm and steady as he spoke.

"When I finally mastered the illusions of Tartarus, it was easier to bear," Rom went on. "But from that point on, I had to endure the fears and nightmares of the prisoners. And some of those were just as haunting, just as vile. I had to listen to their screams, their cries and pleas. Even the most vicious of men, the most ruthless and cutthroat of criminals, would weep like babies when their fears were exposed to them. And it broke me. Just as it broke them."

More tears flowed down Marina's face, but she held her breath, waiting for him to go on.

"And just like you," Rom said, the moisture pooling in his eyes and spilling over onto his face, "I blamed myself. I told myself I deserved every second of that torment. It was the only reason I didn't fight it or try to escape. Because it was my punishment. My penance." He wiped his nose and shook his head. "But neither of us deserves this pain, Marina. You and I deserve to live and to be free. And I know that, together, we can find a way to do that." He paused and took a deep breath. "But we have to forgive ourselves, Marina. We can't carry the burden of guilt and regret like this any longer. We have to move past this and truly free ourselves from this weight. I think that was Tethys's true intention—to break us. To shatter our spirits. And she succeeded. She isolated us. Made us feel alone and unloved for so long." Rom's face crumpled as more tears ran down his face.

Marina leaned forward and pressed her hand against his. "We aren't alone anymore," she whispered through her own tears.

Rom's silver eyes burned in the firelight as he held her gaze. Though his face was stained with tears, there was an intensity in his look that pierced her down to her bones. The same intensity that reminded her of just how powerful he was. His thumb traced absently along the back of her hand, and she suppressed a shudder of pleasure, trying not to envision his fingers touching her elsewhere.

"No, we're not," he murmured. He leaned in and, with his free hand, brushed a tear from the edge of her nose, his touch lingering. Marina's breath caught, her body achingly aware of how close he sat next to her on the log. Close enough to share breath. Close enough to kiss.

"You are worthy of love, Mare," Rom whispered. "You are worthy of a free and happy life. Don't let yourself believe otherwise."

Marina couldn't breathe from the emotion tightening her throat, coiling around her like a serpent. Goddess, this was too much. She didn't deserve to hear this, to share this moment with Rom.

And why not? asked a small voice inside her. *Perhaps I do deserve this. What exactly have I done that is so offensive and horrific as to warrant a cursed life? I shared a night of passion with this man. And that's all. I possess fire magic, but I have never used it to harm someone intentionally. I am Medusa's vessel. But I haven't even embraced my powers yet.*

I am innocent. And I deserve to be free.

As Marina thought these words, something loosened in her chest, releasing the tension she'd carried for years and years. She groaned from the intensity of it as it lifted from her, not realizing how heavy that burden had been until now. Her eyes closed, and she didn't realize she had leaned forward until Rom's forehead pressed against hers. She was panting as if she'd been sprinting, her body beyond exhausted.

"That's it," Rom murmured, his hands now on her

shoulders. "Release it. Let it all go."

Marina swallowed, struggling to find her voice, but all she knew was the roiling emotions burning through her. It was too much. She was floating away, her body weightless. She needed something to ground her, to keep her from disintegrating completely.

Without thinking, she pressed her hands to Rom's cheeks, her fingers brushing against the soft hair of his beard, then running along his full lips. He went perfectly still as her hands explored his face, the length of his nose and cheekbones, his chin and throat. She traced one eyebrow, then the next. Her hands wound through his thick hair, relishing the softness of it. Gradually, her consuming emotions gave way to curiosity and interest as she studied him, noting the silver strands of his hair and the otherworldly glow of his silver eyes. He was a beauty to behold; she couldn't deny it. As much as she wanted to hate him for how devastatingly beautiful he was, she simply... couldn't.

"Why do you call me Mare?" she breathed.

He sucked in a short breath. "What? You don't like it?"

"I like it." She was surprised by the truth of her words. She *did* like it. At first, she'd hated it because it only reminded her of Remy. But the nickname fell so naturally from Rom's lips that it made her blood sing every time he spoke it. And somehow, she knew Remy would've liked Rom. Even if Marina harbored anger and resentment for the lies Remy had told her, she still loved her mother and missed her deeply. "No one but my mother ever called me that before."

Pain flared in Rom's eyes. "I'm sorry—"

Her fingers touched his lips, silencing him. "Don't be. I missed it. And... I like it when you call me that." Her cheeks warmed from the admission.

Desire sparked in his gaze as he leaned closer. "What other names should I call you, Jay?"

Marina smiled. "Only the nice ones, Fox."

"And the naughty ones?"

Flames scorched Marina's blood and bones, making her skin coil with desire. "Especially the naughty ones."

Rom's chuckle rumbled against her. Her hands were still on his face, and she found herself drawing him closer, closer...

Rom suddenly stiffened, his back arching as he released an anguished groan. His breathing turned ragged, his eyes closing in agony.

"Rom?" Marina kept her hands on him, hoping her touch would keep his curse at bay. But the inky black marks appeared on his arms, climbing up and up until they disappeared under his shirt.

Her touch wasn't stopping it. Not this time.

Rom's eyes rolled back, and Marina could only watch helplessly as his curse consumed him.

CHAPTER FIFTEEN

"Rom!" Marina shook him, gripping his shoulders firmly as foam spilled from his lips. His body began to twitch, and his eyes turned all black. Smoke poured from his fingers, wrapping around Marina and creating a foggy haze that obscured the forest from view. The icy chill of death magic swept over her. She remembered how volatile and dangerous his magic had been in the caves in the desert—he'd almost destroyed everyone.

And it was happening again.

"*Rom!*" In an act of desperation, Marina slapped him hard across the face. His head swiveled, and a red mark appeared on his cheek from her strike. But his body was unchanged; the magic was still consuming him.

Panic blurred Marina's thoughts. No, no, no... This couldn't be it. She couldn't lose him. She hadn't even come close to discovering how to break his curse yet. It was too soon.

Her terror melted into rage. Tethys would *not* take him from her. She refused to give up anything else to that damned water goddess. With a growl of determination, Marina climbed onto Rom's lap, bracing her legs on either side of him so their chests were flush against each other. She dug deep within herself and summoned her fire magic. It burned and roiled within her, ready to be unleashed.

Soon, she promised her serpent. *I will let you loose soon. But first, you have to help me save him. Please.*

She wasn't sure if the serpent would respond or not. She wasn't even sure if her serpent was a separate entity or just another version of herself.

But she was desperate. She couldn't lose Rom.

Her fire churned and boiled inside her, and she focused on her palms, narrowing the scope of her magic to those small spaces along her fingertips. With a burst of power, she pressed her hands against Rom's face, channeling all the energy of her fire magic into him. Her skin burned when it touched him, and she felt the searing heat scorching his skin. The smell of burnt flesh met her nose, but she continued to push, prepared to melt the death magic away by force.

"Leave him," Marina hissed. "He is *mine.* He belongs to me."

The death magic raged against her, the smoke thickening into a darkening storm. Lightning flashed, and an otherworldly roar shook the ground. Marina cried out in response, her voice full of fury and venom. She could be powerful and dangerous, too. Let this death magic see how deadly she could become.

She felt her body shifting, morphing. Perhaps the intensity of her rage had conjured her serpent form. But it didn't matter. Her fire was creeping through the darkness, spearing through the dark storm around her. She would tear this force apart. She kept her hands on Rom, her grip on him tightening. His body was quivering underneath her grip, and a low, haunting moan poured from his lips.

"Leave him!" Marina shrieked. Her voice was laced with the hisses of her inner serpent. But something was different. She still felt human. Her hands were still on Rom, her body twined alongside his.

And yet... She could *feel* the presence of her serpent. The hissing, the coiling body, the fangs poised to strike...

Her eyes burned, and she felt an all-consuming power take over her. Her body was lethal. Her gaze was death itself.

She was Medusa incarnate.

She unleashed a feral scream that rang through the night, piercing through the fog of death magic. A blast of fire magic exploded around her, igniting the dark clouds and illuminating the forest clearing. The witches had shifted back to their human forms and looked on with part awe, part terror. Rom's death magic receded, cowering from the brutal power of Marina's magic. His eyes went from black to white. The foam from his mouth cleared, and his body stopped shaking.

Marina closed her eyes as her flames coursed through her, lighting her blood and bones on fire. She felt it everywhere, and she couldn't stop it. Part of her didn't *want* to stop it.

Rom groaned, his body shifting underneath hers, but she kept her eyes shut tight, knowing the story of Medusa and what her penetrating gaze could do to people. She recalled what Hestia had said to her: *Tethys only cursed you with the powers you already have. She's using your magic against you.*

Fire. A serpent's body. The curse of transforming people to stone.

Medusa's powers. But Tethys's curse kept Marina from controlling it properly.

Here and now, for the first time, she wielded all three as Medusa herself. And *she* was in control.

Here and now, her curse was gone. She knew it was only temporary. But the sense of freedom and unparalleled power flowed through her, intoxicating and exhilarating. She felt unstoppable. Unbeatable.

Immortal. Like a goddess.

"Mare..."

Rom's low voice snapped her from her bloodthirsty haze. She kept her eyes closed, her fingers falling from his face so she could wrap her hands around his neck. "Rom. Are you—Are you all right?" Her voice was hoarse from her screams, and the hissing sounds had gone. Did that mean she was human again? Was it safe to open her eyes?

"Gods, Mare..." Rom's hands found hers, his rough callouses scraping along her knuckles. "You—You—"

Marina bit her lip, desperate to look at him, to assess his reaction to her transformation. He must think of her as a monster... And why shouldn't he? That was exactly what she was.

"You're magnificent," he breathed.

Marina's heart lurched. "What?"

"I've never seen anything more beautiful in my entire life."

Marina couldn't breathe. Surely, he couldn't be serious. Medusa? Beautiful? She shook her head, her eyes burning again, but this time with tears. "I can't—I can't be like this. Not around you, not around the witches. It —It isn't safe."

"You are in control, Marina," came Farah's voice from nearby. "It is still *your* body."

Marina tried to focus on her breathing, but she wasn't getting enough air. She couldn't think straight.

All she knew was the flames were still burning her, consuming her, and her fear had overtaken everything. *I can't hurt them. I can't lose anyone else. I can't, I can't, I can't...*

Rom cupped her face in his hands, bringing her forehead against his. "You can do this," he whispered. "You saved me from my god magic. If you can do that, you can do anything. You're so strong, Mare. *You can do this.*"

Marina sniffed and nodded, sucking in deep gulps of air. She counted each breath, slow and steady. When she reached ten, her heart rate had calmed, and she could direct her thoughts again. One breath at a time. Inhale. Exhale.

She focused on her magic. Her serpent. *I will unleash you,* she promised, *if you help me pull this power back.* Once more, she had no idea if her bargaining or pleading made a difference. But she had to try.

Inhale. Exhale. In and out.

Gradually, the fire within her receded, and the cool midnight air nipped at her skin. She felt her skin changing, her body shifting. She hadn't noticed the heavy weight atop her head until it vanished, and she realized her hair had transformed into small snakes. Just like Medusa.

Goddess, what had she looked like? She wished she could see her reflection, but part of her knew it would only disgust her.

And yet... Rom called her beautiful. Magnificent. He was in awe of her appearance.

Perhaps it wasn't as monstrous as she feared.

Rom's thumb swept a tear from her cheek, the gentleness of his touch sending shivers along her spine. "There you are," he murmured. "You can look at me, Mare."

She pressed her lips together and shook her head. "I can't."

"You *can*. It's safe. I swear it."

Marina took a shuddering breath but kept her eyes shut tight. What if he was wrong? What if she would still end up turning him to stone if she looked at him?

"My beautiful goddess, open your eyes," he breathed.

His voice was so tender, so full of emotion and affection, that Marina couldn't stop herself. Her eyes flew open and found Rom's glistening silver gaze boring into hers. He was so close she could taste his breath. Feel his warmth. Their noses brushed as Rom's face split into a wide smile.

"Your eyes are amber," he whispered.

Marina looked him over, inspecting him for injuries. Black marks were etched into his neck and shoulders, obscured by his shirt. But Marina knew they likely covered his entire chest now. The markings stopped just below his chin. It wouldn't be long before they covered his flesh entirely.

Rom's expression sobered as he took in the fear in her eyes. "I'll be fine."

Marina shook her head. "Your magic is getting stronger. I banished it, but it'll only keep coming back until I figure out a way to break your curse."

"It isn't your burden to bear," Rom insisted. "It's my duty to break my own curse. Not yours."

"Hestia's blood has curse-breaking abilities," Marina said. "It *is* up to me."

"I don't want you to risk your life to save me," Rom insisted, his gaze intense as he stared at her. "There are more important things, Mare! You have to save your sisters. You have to defeat the kelpies. And Tethys. Those things are more important than me."

"That's *not true*," Marina snapped. "*You* are important to me, Rom. And I *will not lose you*."

Her voice echoed in the forest, and only then did Marina remember that they weren't alone. The other witches watched them with wide eyes, and even Rom's face went slack with shock at her words. Marina wanted to take them back, to say she didn't mean it, but what good would that do? She was so far from hating him now that there was no use in denying it.

"I will not lose you," she repeated, stroking the dark hair out of his face. "Do not ask me to endure that, Rom. It will be too painful for me to bear."

Rom blinked rapidly, his eyes shining, his face still

blank with surprise and confusion. Had he truly believed she loathed him, this whole time? Had he not understood how she was changing around him? She wished she could make him see, make him understand what he meant to her. But even *she* didn't know the extent of her feelings for him. It was all too confusing, and her body was spent.

The serpent within her hissed, and Marina flinched, drawing away from Rom. She only then realized her legs were still wrapped around him. Her cheeks heated as she extracted herself from him and rose from the log, her legs wobbly. "I—I have to shift now," she muttered, not looking at him. "I trust you can keep yourself alive for the next little while?"

Rom chuckled, but it sounded strained. "Of course."

Marina nodded, still not looking at him, as she unleashed her serpent and shifted, her body elongating along the forest floor. Her thoughts were still on Rom as she slithered away from him.

CHAPTER SIXTEEN

THERE WAS SOMETHING SO *FREEING* ABOUT BEING in her serpent form this time. Marina couldn't explain it. But for the first time, she wasn't shifting out of necessity or survival. She was shifting just because she *could*. Her serpent was at ease. At peace. She knew nothing but bliss.

All the other times she'd shifted had been life-or-death situations. But this... Marina hadn't realized a transition like this was possible. An effortless transformation. Allowing the beast to roam freely, to be free from her cage for the night. A sense of weightlessness settled over her, allowing her to breathe for the first time in fifty years.

She wasn't a slave to her magic. She wasn't running

from her curse. She was merely a snake, slithering along the forest floor. Nothing more. She spent the evening hunting, devouring rodents and birds as she caught them, exploring with her serpent body as she'd never been allowed to before. Occasionally, she caught sight of one of the other witches, also in snake form, but she preferred the solitude. Even so, it was a comfort to know they were there with her.

When her belly was full and her body was weary, she finally coiled within herself to rest. It was a bit unsettling, being unable to close her eyes, but an innate instinct had her closing her retinas so the sights around her wouldn't be a distraction to her always-open eyes. At long last, she succumbed to slumber alongside the soothing sounds of the forest.

"Marina."

Marina's eyes flew open, and she jumped to her feet, immediately disoriented. Her legs were wobbly, and the brightness of daybreak made her squint against the burning sunlight. Panting, she whirled to find Rom standing in front of her, palms raised to indicate he meant no harm.

"Easy," he said. "It's just me."

Marina pressed a hand to her chest, only then realizing she was in her human form. Her cheeks immediately flamed as she expected to find herself naked. But, to her surprise, she was fully clothed, wearing the same blue tunic and tan trousers as the night before. She blinked, stunned that she had not only shifted in her sleep, but she'd managed to conjure her clothes—something she'd never been able to do before.

"You're getting better," Rom said, noticing the same thing. A proud smirk lit up half his mouth, and Marina tried to ignore the way her stomach flipped at the sight.

"What's wrong?" Marina asked, glancing behind him and expecting to find an attacker or assailant or some horrible demon creature chasing after him.

Rom frowned. "Nothing's wrong."

Marina stared at him. "Then, why are you here?" The words were blunt and came across much sharper than she'd intended. When Rom winced, she amended, "I mean, it usually doesn't take long for trouble to find us. I assumed that's why you came to get me."

"No, no, I just—" Rom ran a hand along the back of his neck, and Marina's gaze was drawn to the tattoos covering his arms and neck. Somehow, it only made him look *more* attractive, which hardly seemed fair to her. It also served as a grave reminder of his predicament and their ticking clock. How long before another fit claimed him? How long before his death magic destroyed him entirely?

Rom exhaled slowly through his lips, his cheeks

darkening. For the first time since she'd known him, he seemed... *flustered.* But why? He was always so confident and collected around her, especially when she was unhinged.

"Rom, what is it?" She fought to keep her voice gentle to coax the words out of him, though impatience rattled within her. "Just tell me."

"I thought we could help each other," he said, the words coming out in a rush. "Farah thinks I can train you to use Medusa's powers to locate the other Gorgon sisters, similar to how I used my death magic to locate the kelpies. And, in exchange, I thought maybe we could work on... breaking my curse."

Marina's eyebrows flew upward. "Oh." She bit her lip and dropped her gaze. "I—I'm sorry, Rom, but I really have no idea how to break your curse. If I did, I would've done something by now, I swear—"

"No, I know," Rom said at once. "But Farah seems to think, with you finally tapping into Medusa's magic, that maybe we could... experiment and see what you can do."

Marina arched a single eyebrow. "Experiment?" She didn't like the sound of that.

Rom grinned, looking more like his roguish, handsome self. "Exciting, right? I mean, we already know your touch affects me. I'd like to explore that avenue a bit further." His eyes darkened, and Marina's skin heated at the implication in his words. Goddess, that heady *look* of his was enough to melt her bones right then and there.

Her throat turned dry as she tried to formulate a response. "Sounds dangerous," she finally managed, her voice a bit weak. "What if I hurt you?"

Rom's eyes glinted with mischief. "I like it rough."

Holy shit, the things this man could do to her... Just with his words, she was rendered completely helpless. Her insides turned to mush, her body as useless as if she'd managed to turn herself to stone.

Judging by the way his crooked grin widened at her speechlessness, he was *enjoying* the effect his flirting had on her. Damn him...

Clearing her throat, Marina shifted her weight, achingly aware of every place her clothing touched her skin, itching her flesh. The cotton felt abrasive and restrictive, and she had the sudden desire to shed all her clothing. Perhaps it would've been better if she *had* shifted to her human form without clothing. She now felt like she couldn't breathe with it on.

But the thought of facing Rom without clothes only made her blood boil further, her imagination running wild as she envisioned the ways their bodies could fit together, the sounds she could elicit from him...

Stop it, Marina! She wanted to scream at herself for

being so ridiculous. She crammed her eyes shut and sputtered, "Right. Sure. Sounds good. Let me just—" Her mind was too muddled for her to come up with a valid excuse, so she simply walked away from him, her face on fire, as he chuckled at her blustering idiocy.

CHAPTER SEVENTEEN

After eating some roasted pheasant Dahlia had cooked and washing her face in a nearby stream, Marina finally felt like herself. She wasn't quite ready to face Rom again, knowing he would likely keep teasing her and bringing about those intoxicating feelings she tried so hard to hide from. But she didn't have a choice. Farah wanted to keep moving soon, so she and Rom only had a few minutes to work on their magic before the group set off once more.

Marina and Rom sat side-by-side on the same log from the night before—when Marina had transformed into the embodiment of Medusa and brought Rom back from his death magic.

When he'd called her magnificent. And beautiful.

"You first," Marina said, not quite ready to focus on her intimidating Gorgon powers just yet.

Rom nodded and stretched out his arms to her. For one wild moment, Marina thought he wanted to embrace. But then, his chin dipped, his gaze fixed on the tattoos on his arms. "Can you try to remove these? It's a mark of my death magic. If your magic can erase it, then I think that might buy me more time."

Marina frowned. "Shouldn't I try to break the curse entirely? Buying you more time is just delaying the inevitable."

"One step at a time. I don't think you'll be able to defeat this curse in one attempt. It will take practice. So, let's start with this."

Marina nodded, still frowning. She took one of his hands in hers, allowing her fingers to trace the intricate, swirling design of ink etched into his skin. Her touch trailed up his forearm and elbow, stopping only when he shuddered.

"Sorry," she said quickly, withdrawing her hand. Before she could, he snatched her fingers, keeping her hand pressed against his skin.

"Don't," he murmured, his eyes burning into hers. "It... feels good."

Marina swallowed hard and continued exploring the tattoos along his skin until she reached the cap of his sleeve. "If they weren't a mark of your impending death, I might actually like them. They suit you."

Rom smirked. "Do they? They don't make me look more like a demon?"

Marina looked at him, her expression serious. "You're not a demon, Rom."

Rom snorted. "I'm a prince of Hell. I'm as good as a demon." He cocked his head at her. "Besides, I thought you despised me? Surely calling me a demon isn't the worst of the names you've thought of."

Marina smiled in spite of herself. "True." She took a steadying breath and conjured her fire magic. "I'm starting small, with just a single flame."

"That's fine. You can't hurt me, remember?"

That wasn't entirely true, but Marina remembered pressing a scorching ball of fire into his chest at the inn where the chimera had attacked. Even if it *had* hurt him, his body had healed quickly. Only his shirt had been affected.

Reminding herself of this, she wrapped her fingers around his wrist and focused her flames outward, sending them directly into his flesh. He hissed, his arm stiffening in her grasp, but Marina held fast, feeding more of her fire into him. When she was finished, she released him. A pink imprint of her fingers lingered on his skin before disappearing.

But the black markings were still there.

Marina tried not to be too disappointed. It was only her first attempt, after all.

"Put more power into it," Rom suggested. "I know you're capable of more, Mare. Don't hold back."

Don't hold back. He'd said those same words when they'd made love. Her skin burned from the reminder of that night.

Instead of shying away from those memories, Marina clung to them, allowing them to race along her skin like her flames. Arousal spread through her, making her clench her legs and bite down on her bottom lip. Goddess, she wanted him. She wanted to pin him against a tree and take him right here. She closed her eyes, clasping both his arms, her fingernails piercing his skin. He tensed but didn't object to her fierce grip. Focusing on her inner fire—both her magic and the heat of her memories—Marina pushed more power into Rom. Her insides roared with fury and longing, her serpent coiling inside her, awakened by her anguished desire, her painful yearning, the reminder of all she couldn't have because of this wretched curse.

Rom. All she wanted was Rom. And she could never have him. Like all the other men in her life, he would be ripped away from her. It was too cruel, really—that this god of death had captured her heart so fully. She couldn't turn him to stone, but he was still bound for the Underworld. They could never have a life together.

Swallowing down her grief, Marina pushed harder, fueling her fire with her agony. Her torment. A cry of grief built up in her throat, but she held it back, allowing it to fester inside of her instead. Her eyes pricked with tears. Her serpent longed to be freed, but she coaxed it backward. *Not yet,* she pleaded. *I need you here first.*

The serpent receded, momentarily appeased by her words. But Marina knew she was asking a lot of it, and it would require a release soon. Somehow, she felt in tune with her snake form. It was separate from her, and yet... still a part of her. She couldn't explain it. But she could feel its presence as solidly as she could hear her own thoughts.

Rom groaned, his shoulders slumping slightly, and Marina focused on him, his flesh burning underneath her grasp. With the fire raging inside her, Marina finally concentrated on Medusa's magic—that feeling of utter dominance and power, the unstoppable energy flowing through her. A roar burst from her lips before she could stop it, echoing in the forest. Fire exploded around her, creating a flaming sphere that circled her and Rom, sealing them off from the rest of the world. Rom's back arched as he cried out in pain, but Marina kept going, pushing, pushing, *pushing...*

The fire suddenly died, vanishing entirely, leaving trails of smoke in its wake. Marina sagged backward, blinking spots from her vision, her frame weak from exertion. She closed her eyes and nearly fell unconscious, but a pair of hands grasped her shoulders, holding her upright.

"Mare." Rom's voice was raspy, his breathing ragged. "I've got you."

Dazed, Marina opened her eyes, struggling to focus on his face. But her vision swam, and she could hardly make out the details—he was merely a shapeless form in front of her.

"You did it, Mare. Look."

Squinting, Marina gazed down at his arms. One remained the same, the black markings still etched into his skin. But the other... was completely bare. From his fingertips to his shoulder was nothing but smooth, tan skin.

Marina's mouth fell open, and she swayed. Rom tightened his hold on her shoulders and laughed in amazement. "Gods above, Mare, you *did* it."

CHAPTER EIGHTEEN

Though exhaustion tugged at every part of her body, Marina was itching to do more. Bolstered by her success with Rom, she wanted to use her powers to try locating the other Gorgon sisters.

Rom seemed to read the determined look on her face. He grasped her wrists in his hands. "Mare, don't. You're spent. You need to recover."

"I *need* to find the other Gorgons," Marina insisted. "We're running out of time. What if Tethys has already killed the other fire witches?"

"Then there's nothing you can do for them." Rom's expression was grim.

Marina gritted her teeth and shook her head. "No. That's bullshit. There *is* something I can do. And I'm not going to stop just because I'm a little tired."

"*Mare—*"

Ignoring his protests, Marina flexed her fingers, prepared to summon Medusa's powers again, but a hand fell on her shoulder. She turned and found Dahlia standing next to her, a tentative smile on her face.

"If I may?" she asked, gesturing between Marina and Rom.

Marina found herself nodding, though she had no idea what Dahlia was asking permission to do. Dahlia took one of Rom's hands in hers, then one of Marina's, and pressed them together. Marina tried not to think about how solid and *good* Rom's warm palm felt against hers.

Dahlia's eyes closed, and a trickle of energy crept up Marina's arm, then back down as it funneled into Rom. "You two definitely share an energy," Dahlia murmured, her voice distant. "Power flows between you both. A shared magic."

"The curse," Marina said at once, while Rom nodded.

"Yes." Dahlia dropped their hands, her eyes refocusing on Marina. "I was watching the two of you just now. What you did was impressive, Marina. But I think you're only scratching the surface. This curse binds you both together. I believe Rom can use that shared energy to lend you his strength."

Marina's eyebrows flew upward. "Really?"

"It's a path that runs both ways," Dahlia said. "It's

more powerful on your side because of Hestia's blood. But Rom is still a god, and his strength is... impressive." Her gaze flicked over Rom with approval and something else—something heated. That look sent a jolt of fury coursing through Marina's body.

Rom quirked a single eyebrow but said nothing in response. Marina bit down on a snarl and said, "So what, exactly, are you suggesting?"

"If you want to do more with your magic without exhausting your powers, Rom can lend you his strength," Dahlia said, finally sliding her gaze from Rom to Marina. "But if you continue expending your energy, you'll deplete your strength entirely. An ordinary witch would die from the strain, but for you, you would be rendered unconscious for several days at least."

Marina bit down on her lip, remembering how helpless she'd been after the chimera had wounded her. The sheer shame of having to be carried by Rom made her cheeks burn with embarrassment all over again.

"How would I do this?" Rom asked, his face full of hope.

"Focus on the shared magic between you two," Dahlia instructed. "However that power feels when Marina uses it on you—channel that same power. You have access to it, too. Feed it back to her."

Rom's mouth twisted with doubt, but he shifted on the log so he fully faced Marina. "All right, let's try it."

"What if you hurt me?" Marina couldn't suppress her smirk.

Rom's eyes danced with amusement. "I seem to remember you liking it rough, too."

Marina's skin burned, and she was well aware of Dahlia watching them both. The audacity of flirting with her so blatantly in front of others was both startling and intoxicating. It made Marina wonder what *else* he was willing to do, despite the many witnesses surrounding them.

Rom's hand was still in Marina's, and he took her other hand as well. The smoothness of his warm skin against hers did little to subdue the fire coursing through her—which had nothing to do with her magic and everything to do with the heady look burning in Rom's gaze as he looked at her.

"Don't hold back," Marina murmured.

Rom winked at her—he actually *winked.* Then, he closed his eyes, his grip on her hands tightening. Inky black shadows spread around them, enveloping them, cocooning them in a smoky barrier that cut them off from the outside world. Even Dahlia was obscured from view as Rom's death magic swirled around them.

"Focus on the power you share with Marina," Dahlia said, her voice sounding farther away than before. "Your death magic wants to take over, but don't let it. This is a separate power. Something only you and Marina share."

Something only we share. Marina had never thought of her curse as something to appreciate, but in this moment, it didn't seem so terrible to share this with Rom—a power only they had access to. Magic they could wield together.

Rom's arms shook, and Marina let her thumb graze his in a subtle gesture of encouragement. *You can do this, Rom.*

Rom took a deep, steadying breath, and then the air shifted. The shadows stopped swirling, and something else filled the space between them. It smelled of mint and wood smoke and had a unique musky scent that was distinctly Rom. It reminded her of that night they shared together.

The night that had changed everything.

Marina had always thought it was her own arousal, her own selfish and lustful thoughts that betrayed her when she thought of that night. She was weak, and she yearned for Rom's body. That was all.

But for the first time, she considered an alternative. Perhaps the reason she kept thinking of that night wasn't because of her arousal; perhaps it was because that was the moment the magic between them first merged. That night, the convergence of their bodies marked the beginning of their curse and, therefore, the beginning of the magic that flowed between them.

And now, years later, whenever they used this power

together, Marina was brought back to the beginning. Was it the same for Rom? Did he remember that night, too?

Fire rose up inside her in response to the magic churning around them. Marina didn't want to suppress it like she'd done for most of her life, but she also didn't want to unleash it when Rom was working on his powers. At any rate, her body still felt fragile after expending so much energy earlier. Instead, she sat there, still and silent, and let the powers flow freely through her. She wouldn't unleash it, but she wouldn't stop it, either. The fire was a part of her. It *was* her. Just as Hestia had said.

Rom grunted with exertion, his hands trembling as he held onto Marina's. She squeezed his fingers in response.

"Don't force it," Dahlia said. "The door is open. All you have to do is walk through."

Rom's grip relaxed slightly, but his hands were still trembling.

Come on, Rom, Marina thought, trying to maintain steady breaths.

The air shifted again, and Marina felt a foreign power enter her body. She gasped as an intensity of magic jolted through her, sizzling her skin and bones. Once more, she was taken back to the temple when Rom had first entered her body. The sheer awareness of it all, the sensation of him filling her completely, returned to her. Sweat formed along her brow, and her thighs clenched with need. Goddess, it felt *so powerful.* It actually felt like they were naked and he was thrusting into her. The sensation was so raw, so feral and *real* that Marina almost cried out from the ecstasy of it all.

"That's it," Dahlia urged, and her voice pierced through the fog of Marina's passion, sending momentary clarity to her mind.

Focus, Mare, she ordered herself. She blinked rapidly, trying to stay anchored in this moment instead of drifting off into her fantasies of Rom's naked body entwined with hers. The awareness of his magic coursed through her, lighting her veins on fire. Her magic exploded with strength and power, bursting inside her. Before she could stop herself, the flames roared to life, consuming her body and wrapping her flesh in liquid fire. Dahlia yelped and jerked backward, but Rom tightened his hold on Marina's wrists, keeping their connection intact.

"Let go!" Marina cried. "Rom, I'm burning you!"

"No! I'm not done yet!" Rom's voice was strained, his arms shaking more violently. Marina's fire swirled, scorching and intense, heating the space between them. Goddess, she would melt his flesh right off his bones if he didn't let go.

With a shout, Rom finally released her, slumping

backward. As soon as the connection between them was broken, Marina's flames subsided, and the black smoke vanished. She lunged forward, catching Rom by the shoulders before he fell backwards onto the forest floor. His face was deathly pale, and shadows lined his eyes. His arms were still shaking.

Dahlia helped Marina slide Rom off the log, propping him up against it so he didn't fall over. "By the Goddess," Dahlia murmured, wiping sweat from her brow. "That was incredible. I've never seen such power before." She was watching Rom with that infuriating look in her eyes again.

Marina wanted to rip her head off for that look, but she swallowed down a nasty remark, remembering that without Dahlia's help, they wouldn't have succeeded. She felt rejuvenated, as if she'd just woken up from a restful night's sleep. As if she hadn't expended all of her magic earlier.

Meanwhile, Rom looked like he was on the brink of death itself.

"Thank you," Marina forced herself to say. "I—I didn't realize we were capable of sharing power like that."

Dahlia nodded. "Curses are tricky things. They entrap us, but they can also empower us. Magic goes both ways."

Marina nodded, wondering if Tethys had considered

this when she'd cursed them both. If she truly wanted to punish them, she wouldn't have knowingly granted them this shared power. No, there was no way she'd known. The thought send a flare of triumph inside Marina's chest. This was yet another advantage they had over the water goddess.

Perhaps there was a way for them to defeat her after all.

"Did it work?" Rom asked, his voice a low rasp.

Marina took his hand again, and it felt colder than before. "Yes. It worked."

"Find them, Mare. I know you can do it." Rom leaned his head back against the log, closing his eyes.

Marina looked up at Dahlia, who nodded encouragingly. It was time to locate the other Gorgons.

Taking a deep breath, Marina released Rom's hand—not wanting to injure him further—and conjured Medusa's power. That same strength—Rom's strength—flowed through her, fueling her magic. A low hiss burned in her throat. She felt her body shifting, morphing into Medusa's form. She shut her eyes tight, not wanting to turn Dahlia or Rom into a block of stone. Now that she was focused on it, she could sense the change in her hair. It was *moving*. And it was much heavier than before.

Snakes. There were *snakes* growing from her scalp. The thought made Marina feel ill, but she tried not to dwell on it. *It's no different from shifting to your serpent form,* she reminded herself. It was merely a variation of her usual shift.

Marina focused her energy inward, delving deeply into herself. She tunneled so far into her magic that she found herself face-to-face with its source: the soul of Medusa. It burned bright within her, like a beacon urging her onward. Fury and flames and unstoppable power.

"Show me your sisters," Marina whispered to it.

The soul of Medusa flickered like the flame of a candle. Then, it surged forward, bursting from within Marina's chest. It speared outward, jutting through the forest and winding through the trees. Marina followed its path, feeling oddly disconnected from her body as she trailed after Medusa's aura. She was floating, her own soul detached from her body as she soared alongside Medusa like a ghost. They weaved through trees and boulders, mountains and rivers, finally settling on a cave etched into the side of the Emdale Mountains. Medusa's spirit hovered above a form chained to the cave wall, her wrists raw and bleeding from her restraints. Her black hair was matted and filthy, and her emerald eyes shone even in the darkness.

She looked like Marina. Pale skin, black hair, green eyes... A fire witch just like her. Never in her life had

Marina met someone who shared her features, least of all a fire witch.

Medusa's spirit jumped to the opposite cave wall where a similar figure was chained, this one unconscious, her head lolled to the side. She, too, had black hair, but half her head was shaved, exposing scars and bloody wounds along her scalp.

My sisters. Marina couldn't believe it. They were here. They were *real.*

Medusa's sisters. The three Gorgons, reunited.

Something shifted in the darkness, and Marina caught sight of several dark figures moving toward the chained women. Gravel and dirt shifted, and the huge shape of a horse came into view.

Kelpies. They were made of rock and stone, the sound of crunching pebbles echoing in the cave as they moved. One of them emitted a low whinny, as if they were speaking to one another. Marina strained to understand it, to figure out what they were saying...

In a flash, one of the kelpies turned its head and looked directly at Marina. The kelpie's eyes glowed gold, and a growl built up in its throat.

Marina's panic took over, and her body jerked. Something heavy slammed into her. Her eyes opened. Gravity pressed in on her, choking the breath out of her. Spots danced in her vision and she hunched over with a groan, clutching her side as she struggled to breathe.

She was back in the woods, sitting on the log, her mind returning to the present. Medusa's spirit vanished, leaving Marina disoriented and dizzy.

"Mare? Mare!" Rom's hands were on her, trying to keep her upright just as she'd done with him earlier. "What happened?"

The other witches had gathered around them while Marina's mind had been traveling with Medusa's spirit. They watched her with anxious anticipation.

Marina rubbed her chest, finally finding her voice. "I —I found them. The Gorgons. The kelpies have them." She looked at Farah, whose jaw was taut with determination. "They're in the Emdale Mountains."

Farah nodded once. "Then we are on the right path. Come, we've no time to waste."

Marina rose to her feet, her head throbbing from the movement as she took Farah's arm. "That's not all. The kelpies... they saw me. They *recognized* me." A cold tendril of dread worked its way into her chest, her skin prickling with the awareness of something dark headed toward her. "They are coming."

CHAPTER NINETEEN

THE WITCHES SPRANG INTO ACTION.

Marina unsheathed her blades as Rom appeared beside her, a fierce expression on his face. Farah shouted orders to the others. Seven witches formed a circle, clasping hands as they chanted a protection spell. The remaining witches shifted to their serpent forms. Marina glanced down at the dagger hilts clutched in her palms, feeling for the first time that her instinct *wasn't* to wield knives but to wield her fire magic.

Save it, she told herself. *Save your powers for when you truly need them. Don't expend all your energy right away.* Her serpent writhed inside her, and she mentally cursed herself. She'd promised to free the serpent, to allow it freedom in exchange for help channeling Medusa's magic.

But something told her the snake would get its wish shortly. The kelpies wouldn't be defeated so easily.

"Remember, they *can* be killed, if only temporarily," Farah called out as a reminder to the witches. "It will buy us enough time to escape." The ground began to tremble, and Farah's eyes widened. "Ready yourselves!"

Marina gritted her teeth, raising her hands in preparation. From the ground, great creatures rose up, made of a combination of rock and soil. A loud roar shook the branches around them, and it took all of Marina's willpower not to stagger back a step from the sheer intensity of it.

In an instant, a dozen kelpies stood before them, and Marina felt her blood ice over. These were different. They stood twice as tall as the previous kelpies, their glowing gold eyes roving over the witches as if they were nothing more than ants to trample.

They were *massive.* Some were formed of rocks and pebbles, others from soil and thick, sturdy roots. These weren't the malleable sand creatures from before. These were *stronger.*

Far less easy to kill.

Marina glanced around, taking in the fear in the other witches' faces as they registered the same realization. But she wouldn't be cowed. She wouldn't let this deter her.

These monsters had stolen her kin—the fire witches

and the Gorgons. They were demons who needed to be destroyed.

With a feral roar, Marina lunged, allowing her fury to fuel her as she charged. The beasts shrieked in response, meeting her head-on. Marina ducked before one of them crashed into her, then sliced at one of its hooves, severing it from the body. It didn't bleed, of course, but it did slow down, its balance thrown off as the leg reformed from the soil in the ground. Marina took advantage of its lapse in concentration and plunged her dagger into its throat, slicing hard to the left, cutting through roots and stones. But the blade wouldn't cut through it easily. Marina cried out as her knife got stuck, and no amount of tugging could pull it free.

"*Shit!*" she screamed. The kelpie's leg had healed, and he snapped its teeth at her. Marina barely dodged its strike, forced to abandon her knife to save herself. Their bodies were too dense. Too indestructible. She would need something far stronger than a small dagger to kill these creatures.

Beside her, Rom struck at the kelpies again and again with his death magic, his black smoke coiling around their bodies before slashing straight through them. Hope flared in Marina's chest as she watched his magic spear directly into the kelpie's chest.

Yes, she thought in triumph. *Rom is a death god. If anyone can kill them, it's him.*

They had a fighting chance after all.

But as Marina watched the dark vapor surround the kelpies, a tendril of dread formed in her chest. The kelpies were unaffected by Rom's magic. If anything, they seemed to be... *inhaling* it. Slowly, the black smoke vanished, and the kelpies' gold eyes flashed. They unleashed an almighty roar of power, and Marina swore they rose several inches in height.

Rom's arms dropped, his eyes wide with horror as he stumbled backward. His magic was *feeding* the creatures.

Marina was running for him before she could think. Rom was too stunned to notice one of the kelpies careening toward him. Marina tackled him to the ground, narrowly avoiding getting trampled by the kelpie. They collided against the forest floor, roots and thorns scraping their flesh. Marina grunted, her skin stinging from the impact.

"Mare," Rom groaned, his face pale.

Marina climbed off him and helped him to his feet. "Are you all right?"

"How?" Rom asked weakly. "How are they immune to my magic?"

"Tethys may have created them, but she used *your* magic to do it," Marina said, shaking her head in disbelief. "It must have been something from what you did earlier, in the desert, when you banished them. You—

Your magic is *linked* to them, Rom. It's a part of them now."

Terror marred his features as he gaped at Marina. "No," he breathed, gazing around the forest as the witches fought the kelpies, some as serpents and others in their human forms. "Mare, they can't—"

A high-pitched scream cut through his words, and Marina whirled to find Wren battling two kelpies. Inky black smoke swirled around her, obscuring her from view.

"Oh, Goddess, no," Marina whispered, rushing forward. But she was too late. Wren's scream grew more and more distant, and when the smoke faded from view, the fire witch had vanished.

Marina stopped, her blood running cold. "What the hell just happened? Where did she go?" Panic rose in her chest as she scanned the forest. But Wren was nowhere to be found.

"They banished her," Rom choked. "They—They used *my power.*"

The same power he'd used in the caves in the desert. The kelpies had absorbed the magic and used it against them.

"Goddess help us," Marina murmured, her voice trembling.

Rom met her gaze, determination bleeding through

his fear and disbelief. Slowly, he nodded, and Marina knew what he was telling her.

The time was now.

Marina didn't hesitate. She spread her arms, unleashing an unholy shriek of power and fury as she shifted, allowing Medusa to take over. Flames sprang to life, coursing up and down her body. A heavy weight bore down on her scalp as her hair turned into serpents, her body elongating and stretching as she grew several feet in height, now matching the height of the kelpies. She surged forward, her feet leaving the forest floor as she floated toward the closest creature. With a slash of her arms, she cut right through the horse's throat, leaving a path of flames across its body.

The kelpie roared, rearing back as rocks and pebbles poured from its wound like droplets of blood. Marina struck again, embedding her hand into its chest until she gripped the heart of the creature and squeezed tightly. With an anguished scream, the kelpie disintegrated in a puff of dust and dirt.

From behind, she sensed Rom covering her, fighting off other kelpies trying to reach her. Marina was amazed and enthralled by the lithe way he moved, his powerful body striking blow after blow with his fists. His magic couldn't kill them, but he could certainly hold them off with brute strength while Marina took them out one at a time.

But it wasn't enough.

More screams filled the air. One by one, the kelpies banished the fire witches. Dahlia was next, her cries echoing as she vanished in a whirlwind of black smoke.

Marina let loose a shout of rage as she moved faster, struck harder, her body moving with lethal grace. Her furious gaze bore into the golden eyes of the kelpie closest to her, and it stilled, turning into stone, its body frozen mid-strike. While her magic held it, Marina crushed its body, and it crumbled at her feet.

She was powerful, but she was only one person. One soldier. They were still vastly outnumbered, and the witches were vanishing despite her best efforts.

She couldn't save them. The knowledge burrowed deep inside her, festering like an angry wound as Marina fought and fought, letting her anger fuel her. But anger made way for despair and devastation as her sisters continued to disappear.

Soon, only Farah remained. Her grim gaze rested on Marina for a heartbeat as a kelpie galloped toward her.

"Don't give up!" Farah called to her. "You can still win this war, Marina. We're all counting on you." Her gaze was full of fire and steel as the kelpie reached her, its dark smoke whipping toward the coven leader and enveloping her completely. Farah didn't scream, but her face was taut with agony as the death magic consumed her.

Marina cried out, reaching helplessly toward Farah as she disappeared. The mighty coven leader, the strong and capable fire witch, was gone. Not even *she* could stop the kelpies.

Marina fought to keep from crumpling, from sinking into hopelessness. If Farah couldn't fight this, then how could she? It was only her and Rom now. Seven kelpies remained, and they closed in on the two of them, their eyes flaring hungrily.

Those beasts, those savage demons, had stolen Marina's friends.

This is it, Marina thought, allowing her rage to bleed through her anguish. One way or another, it would end here.

She glanced at Rom, whose jaw was rigid, his silver eyes flashing. He raised his hands, and thunder crackled around them. Shadows poured from his fingertips, coating the forest floor and surrounding the last remaining kelpies.

Marina crouched low, pressing her hands into the ground. Flames erupted around them, igniting the shadows and forming a wall of fire. Several kelpies whinnied in alarm, rearing backward, away from the fire. But Rom continued feeding his shadows to the flames, and Marina pushed harder with her fire, allowing it to burn freely.

Like before, their shared magic converged, forming

something new. Something deadly. It wasn't just death magic and fire magic anymore. It was a new power that the kelpies couldn't defeat.

One of the kelpies—made entirely of tree roots—caught fire, roaring in pain. Marina struck that one first, severing its head completely. She didn't wait for it to crumble before she moved on to the next one. Rom assaulted each kelpie with more of his shadows, blinding them, fueling Marina's fire, which seemed to be their weakness.

Of course it was. These creatures were created by Tethys, and Marina's power was created by Hestia. They were opposites.

That knowledge spurred Marina onward as she flung more and more of her fire toward the kelpies. Their strangled shrieks pierced the air, echoing around her, and she reveled in it. Let them suffer. Let them perish for what they had done to the fire witches.

They would pay for their crimes. The fire witches would never be hunted by these creatures again.

Marina stretched her arms wide, unleashing a scream that ripped from her throat, tearing her body apart as she exploded, her power bursting, igniting the entire forest in unholy flames. White-hot light blinded Marina, filling her vision, consuming her senses. She gave herself over to the magic completely, leaving nothing left. Even if it killed her, she would end these creatures forever.

Rom's shout of warning was the last thing she heard before darkness took her.

CHAPTER TWENTY

Marina was warm. Too warm. Slowly, she blinked, her eyes as crusty as if she'd been asleep for a full week. Her body ached and throbbed from head to toe, but she forced herself to a sitting position. She expected to find herself in the same forest she'd been in before, but her surroundings were different. There were sparse trees, but mostly rocks and boulders. Ahead of her loomed the massive peak of the Emdale Mountains.

She was at the base of the mountains. How?

"You're up."

Marina whirled to find Rom approaching. He ran a hand through his wet hair, and flecks of water dripped down his face. His shirt was open down to his collarbone, revealing a mass of dark chest hair.

"You're... wet," Marina said blankly, her cheeks instantly heating from her words.

Rom smirked. "I found a river nearby and took the time to clean myself. I was starting to smell."

Marina arched an eyebrow. "So you just left me here on my own, unconscious?"

Rom snorted. "You're hardly helpless, Mare. I knew if anyone dared approach you, your Medusa powers would protect you. Even if you're unconscious, the spirit of Medusa lives inside you. I don't think she'd allow anything or anyone to sneak up on you."

Marina's mouth twisted into a scowl. She wasn't so sure about that. If a kelpie had come for her—

Her heart stuttered with realization. She rose to her feet, her head spinning. "The kelpies—"

"You killed them all," Rom said solemnly. "They're gone. And that forest... Well, it burned to the ground. But that was unavoidable." He shrugged as if it were no great loss. "I managed to drag you out of the forest before the fire took us both."

Killed them all. Shock numbed her body. She thought she would feel regret for unleashing so much horror and destruction, for leveling an entire forest. But she didn't. If anything, she wished she'd been conscious to witness the kelpies' deaths. "All of them?" she asked. When Rom nodded, she asked, "But won't they come back? Farah said we could only kill them temporarily."

"No, they are well and truly dead. I can sense it with my magic. You used Hestia's power to defeat them, Marina."

Marina's mouth fell open as she remembered Farah's words: *Only the power of a goddess can destroy them for good.* And if she had used the magic of Hestia—the fire goddess—then perhaps they *were* truly dead.

"I'm sure there are a few left, guarding their prisoners," Rom went on. "But they won't dare come after us. Trust me. You made an impression, Mare."

Marina should have been proud and triumphant as Rom clearly was. But all she felt was guilt and regret. It filled her chest, nearly consuming her. "It was my fault." Her voice was hollow and barely above a whisper.

Rom frowned. "What was your fault?"

"The kelpies. They only came for us because they found me when I was searching for the Gorgons. They were here for *me*."

"They would have found the witches eventually," Rom said. "That's their mission—to hunt down the fire witches until there are no more left. It isn't your fault that they did what they were created to do."

Marina shook her head, his words rolling off her like they meant nothing. "If I hadn't cast that damn spell, this wouldn't have happened!"

"Yes, and then you wouldn't have known where your

Gorgon sisters were," Rom argued. "It was necessary, Marina. It had to be done."

"At what cost?" Marina's voice rose in volume. "What if the fire witches are dead because of it? Farah and Wren... Dahlia..." She broke off on a choke, her eyes burning.

"Mare. *Mare.*" Rom was in front of her then, his hands on her shoulders as he forced her to meet his gaze. "Don't do this. Don't let your guilt take over. You still have a mission to fulfill. We can save them."

Anger roared inside her, and she shoved him hard in the chest until he stumbled back a step. "What do *you* care? You're only here to break your curse! You don't care about them at all!"

Rom's eyes flared with part indignation, part fury. "I *do* care! They took me in when no one else would. They're my family, too, Marina."

"Bullshit! You're only here because you had no other choice! It was *your* power that the kelpies used to banish them. This is *your* fault as much as it is mine."

Horror and anguish filled his face. For the briefest of seconds, Marina regretted inflicting that pain on him, but she shoved the thought away, letting her rage take over. "In fact, *all* of this is your fault. You banished the witches in the first place. Your very presence brought the damn kelpies to our doorstep. You *cursed* me! This is *all* because of you, Rom."

Devastation burned in his gaze as he stepped back again, panting as if her accusations were physical blows. His eyes closed, his expression crumpling. Marina's words echoed around them, and she couldn't take them back. Now that they were spoken, her chest deflated, her anger leaving almost instantly.

She'd broken Rom. She'd flung her words at him, the very words she meant to direct toward herself.

It wasn't his fault at all. She knew that. But the shame on his face told her he was just like her: quick to loathe himself. Quick to believe the lie that it was all his fault. He wore the burdens just as she did. He shouldered the blame, allowing it to drag him down even if it killed him.

They were so much alike. Marina hadn't allowed herself to see it until now.

"Rom." She took a step toward him, but he raised a hand to stop her, shaking his head slightly, his face still contorted with despair so potent that Marina's chest ached.

"Don't," he said in a strangled voice. "You're—You're right. This is all my fault. All my fault." His voice faded into a whisper, his eyes glistening with tears as he turned away from her.

Oh, Goddess, what have I done? "Rom!" Marina strode after him, determined not to let him walk away with her horrible insults still pulling him down. She had to fix this, to make this right.

She reached out to grasp his shoulder, and he suddenly went stiff, his back arching as he cried out in pain.

"Oh, shit," Marina whispered. His curse was trying to claim him. And her magic was spent. What if she couldn't bring him back? She grabbed his shoulders, spinning him around so he faced her. His eyes rolled back, and his muscles strained, his body jerking at odd angles. "Rom! *Rom!*" Marina shook him violently, despite knowing it would do no good. Her touch had been enough before, but the death magic was fighting harder now. She would need to do more.

She reached out for her fire magic, for Medusa's essence inside her, but both were silent. Unmoving. Unresponsive. "Come on!" she growled. "I need you!"

A tiny voice inside her murmured, *I will do you no more favors... until you free me.*

Marina's skin chilled from the words. Her serpent. She'd made it wait for too long, and now, it was abandoning her. If she lost Rom because of her stubborn, infuriating snake, then she'd—

No. She cut off that line of thinking before it took over. She would *not lose Rom.*

Gritting her teeth in determination, Marina stepped

forward, pressing both hands to Rom's face and pinching him there. "Wake up, you bastard! You're stronger than this!" She was tempted to slap his face, hoping to snap him out of it, but she'd tried that last time, and it hadn't worked. Wracking her brain, she unleashed a scream of frustration. "I *can't lose you*, Rom! Not until I make things right. Not until I make you see that you're innocent in all this, just like me. We are together in this curse. And I'll be damned if I let it take you from me." She drew even closer, an insane idea taking root in her mind.

It's worth a shot, she told herself. She would do anything to save him.

So, she brought his face to hers and pressed a kiss to his mouth.

She felt completely idiotic, kissing this man when he was in the throes of a fit, when he was on the brink of death. But if her touch could bring him back—if their passionate night together was the trigger, then perhaps something akin to passion would be enough to bring him back.

Going back to the beginning, she thought, her lips moving over his with fervent energy. *When you first captured my heart.*

Marina could have sworn Rom's body went still when she kissed him. Encouraged by this, she grabbed the collar of his shirt to pull him closer. Nothing was happening. But he wasn't trembling violently anymore.

She belatedly remembered the foam that often poured from his mouth… but she didn't taste anything except *him.* That delicious taste she clung to in her memories. But they didn't do him justice at all. He tasted *divine.* Like lust and power wrapped together in something smoky.

"Rom," she murmured against his lips.

And his lips responded to hers—with slow movements at first. His breath hitched, and a low groan rumbled in his throat. Then, his mouth was on fire, claiming hers again and again. A flick of his tongue, and Marina was completely undone.

Goddess. She moaned in his mouth, and he captured that, too, his hands finding her waist and pinning his hips to hers. Together, they backed up until Marina was pressed against the sturdy trunk of a tree. Rom ground into her, his kisses lighting a path of fire along her skin.

"Gods, Marina," he whispered. "I've wanted to do this from the moment I first saw you in that cave."

Thank the Goddess, she thought, overcome with a mixture of desire and gratitude. *It worked. He's back. He's here with me again.*

Rom opened his mouth to speak, but Marina silenced him with another kiss, her body unraveling inch by inch with every place he touched her, everywhere his skin met hers.

Rom broke away again, his silver eyes glittering, and

Marina was so relieved that he had returned to her that at first she didn't process that he was speaking to her.

"All those years—all that time away from you—and all I wanted was to come back to you," he breathed. "I would have given *anything* to come back to you, Mare. You were on my mind. Constantly. I've only ever been yours. For the rest of my existence, it will only ever be *you*."

Marina's blood heated from his admission, her throat closing, her breath catching. She didn't know how to respond. It was too much... The heat of him against her, his urgent kisses, and then *this*.

But if she was being honest with herself, he'd consumed her mind just as she'd consumed his. She couldn't deny it any longer.

"You have no idea how much you've haunted me," she said in a strained voice, the confession causing her physical pain. Her chest tightened, squeezing the life out of her, but she had to get it out. She had to make him understand. "You've ruined me forever, Romanos. Because no one and nothing will ever compare to you." Tears burned her eyes, but she pushed onward. "I loathed you when you first came back, not because of the curse, but because of how the memory of you tormented me day after day. And then you had the gall to *show up* and upend my life all over again." Tears streamed down her face. "Regardless of my curse, I was certain I would never find love. Not after you."

Rom's eyes shone with tears, and he pressed his forehead to hers with another groan. "Mare." He said the word like a plea, as if he couldn't manage to say anything else.

"You aren't allowed to leave me, you understand?" Marina said, trying to put as much authority into her voice as possible. "You are *mine*. And you aren't going anywhere. We're cursed together. And together, we'll be freed. Got it?"

A weak chuckle escaped his lips. "Got it."

CHAPTER TWENTY-ONE

As they ascended the mountain hand-in-hand, Marina focused on the soothing feel of his palm pressed against hers, as if it had always belonged there. She thought of the lightness in her chest, the way she could suddenly breathe as if her lungs had been blocked for fifty years.

But it was all a distraction. Because Marina couldn't ignore the fact that the tattoos now covered every inch of Rom's skin. He must've had another fit while she'd been unconscious. The black swirls had climbed up his neck, now curving along his cheeks and forehead and the back of his neck. Even the markings she'd managed to erase with Medusa's power had returned.

He was out of time. There was nowhere left for the death magic to mark him.

We're in this together, Marina reminded herself. *I won't let it take him.* If his death magic tried to claim him, she would use Medusa's powers again. She would stop it.

When they reached the first peak, they made camp for the night. Marina shifted to her serpent form, allowing the creature its freedom just in case she needed its powers again soon. The snake was seething, hissing and spitting in anger as it took over her body.

I know, Marina told it. *I'm sorry. I'll do better next time.*

In her defense, a lot had happened in the past few days. But one thing she was learning with her magic was that it was a separate entity. As Farah had told her, it was still *her* body. But she was sharing it with another soul.

Medusa's soul.

She wasn't sure if this meant Medusa *was* the serpent, or if it had its own unique soul. But Marina was too tired to think it over, so she surrendered her mind to the serpent as she slithered along the rocky expanse of the mountain. There weren't many animals for her to hunt, but she did manage to kill and devour a small mouse. That would suffice for now.

She expected to spend the night in the serpent's body. But to her surprise, after a few hours, the snake retreated, and her human form returned, fully clothed like before. She shook off the lingering disorientation from being in an animal's body before she climbed down from the boulders the snake had scaled and made her way back to Rom.

He'd started a fire and was standing next to the flames, arms crossed and shivering. His face was pale, and dark shadows lined his eyes.

He was dying. Marina couldn't deny it any longer. He looked as if a violent plague were about to claim his life at any moment.

Rom quirked a wry grin in her direction. "I know. I look terrible."

Marina's throat tightened as she drew closer to stand next to him. "Rom—"

"Just promise me you'll keep going," he said, his teeth chattering. "You can still save them, Mare. It's always been you. *You* are the key to their freedom."

Marina was shaking her head. "I refuse to lose you, Rom."

Rom sighed. "You are formidable and powerful, Marina. But I think this is beyond you now. It's beyond both of us." His eyes met hers. "But thank you for keeping me alive this long. I wouldn't have made it this far without you."

Marina's nostrils flared as she closed the distance between them. "Don't you *dare* say your goodbyes as if you're giving up. I thought you were better than that."

Rom spread his arms. "What else can we do? The magic of the Underworld is too strong, even against both of us." He shook his head in despair. "It's everything I deserve."

"*No!*" Marina barked, pressing her hands to his cheeks and forcing him to meet her gaze. "All those terrible things I said to you... I didn't mean them, Rom. I was thinking of myself. *I'm* to blame for this, and I lashed out at you. It wasn't fair of me. But *none* of this is your fault."

"I was living the life of a god in the Underworld while you were suffering," Rom argued.

"*You* were suffering, too! You lived in Tartarus, for Goddess's sake!"

"But I was never in any danger. My magic was strong, and I still had privileges. But you—"

Marina pressed her fingers to his lips, silencing him. "We were both suffering, Rom. We were both victims. But we're stronger now for it. Do not let Tethys win! We can still fight her together! You saw how unstoppable we were against those kelpies. I *need* you. You make me stronger, Rom. You make me more powerful."

Rom's eyes closed, and a single tear streaked a path down his face. "You don't need me."

"Don't tell me what I need," Marina growled. She kissed him, hard and unyielding, and he grunted in surprise. When she pulled away, he only brought her in again for another kiss, softer this time, his lips smooth and gentle.

But Marina didn't want gentle. Gentle was feeble. It was the sensation of one who had given up.

And she needed Rom to *fight*.

She bit down on his lower lip, and he gasped. Her tongue slid between his lips, twining with his. He groaned, his body arching into her, and she felt his hardness pressing against her.

"Come on, Rom," she whispered into his mouth. "Show me you're willing to fight. Don't hold back on me. Not now." She tugged at his trousers until his hips were flush against hers.

"Gods, Mare," he rasped. His hands wound around the back of her neck, bringing her face to his again, his fingertips running a path through her hair and sending delicious shivers up and down her spine.

"You are a death god," Marina whispered. "Show me how powerful you can be."

Rom withdrew, his eyes darkening with need and intensity. For a moment, they stared at each other breathlessly. The air between them felt charged with something potent, something tangible that Marina wanted to explore.

And then, it erupted between them. Rom was kissing

her, his mouth trailing down her neck and finding her collarbone. He slid her shirt to the side so he could suck on her shoulder, his tongue moving lower and lower. Fabric ripped, and Marina's shirt fell to pieces around them. Then, her undershirt was gone, and Rom's hands cupped her breasts, tracing circles around her peaked nipples. She cried out with delight as she tore his shirt off him, allowing her hands to roam the hardened, muscular planes of his chest. Every inch of his skin was marked by the inky black swirls, but it only aroused her further. They were the markings of his power. He looked like a hardened, weathered soldier, the tattoos telling a story of his pain and suffering—and how he would emerge victorious from it all.

"You're beautiful," she whispered.

Rom's gaze ignited as he brought her body against his, her nipples rubbing against his chest. His hands tugged at her trousers until they dropped to the ground. Then, his fingers ran between her thighs, rubbing along the wetness collecting there. Marina writhed against his hand, urging him onward. He inserted one finger, then two, and she gasped, her mind spiraling. Her knees buckled, and she would have collapsed to the ground if he hadn't had his free hand bracing her back, keeping her upright. His fingers curled inward, brushing against her inner walls, pumping faster and faster. Stars burst in her vision, and she was on the brink of coming undone, of unraveling completely.

Too soon, Rom removed his hand, and Marina growled at him, desperate for release.

"Not yet," he murmured in her ear. "I want to set you on fire first."

Marina wanted to argue that she was already there, that she was burning for him now, but she held her tongue, instead focusing on his trousers. They came undone, and his length sprang free, hard and slick with need. Marina ran her hand along his arousal, and he hissed a curse.

"Perhaps I'll set *you* on fire," she murmured, her hand gliding up and down his length.

"*Shit,* Mare." Rom pressed his forehead against hers, his grip tightening along her hips, his fingers pressing hard into her flesh, no doubt leaving bruises there.

But Marina wanted the pain. She wanted him to be rough with her.

She tugged him downward until they both collapsed to the ground. The rocks were cool to the touch, the sharpened edges biting into Marina's naked skin, but she relished the feeling, relished the pain. She wanted to *feel.* She wanted the intensity of it to mark her forever.

The fire crackled beside them as Rom hovered over her, bracing his arms on either side of her.

"I want you," she told him. "Hard and fast. I want to forget my own name. Give me everything, Rom."

"Yes, my goddess." Rom's mouth was on her throat, his teeth scraping along her neck, and she shuddered underneath him. His breath tickled her skin as he whispered, "But only if you come undone for me."

"Yes," she gasped.

His hips ground into her as he nudged at her entrance. She wrapped her legs around his middle, urging him closer. With one swift movement, he thrust into her, and she cried out as he filled her completely. Their one night together hadn't been nearly enough. She felt all the satisfaction of that night and so much more, his body entwining so perfectly with hers. He pulled back, then slammed into her again.

She bit down on his shoulder. "Harder," she commanded.

"Make me," he groaned. "Burn, Marina. Burn for me. Show me how powerful you can be."

He pounded into her again, and she screamed into the night as pleasure and pain mingled with each thrust.

"Burn, Marina," he repeated.

And she obliged. She unleashed everything with another scream, her serpent and fire magic exploding within her. Medusa's powers ignited, setting her body aflame. She almost cried out in surprise and alarm, worried she'd hurt him and burn him alive, but Rom didn't complain. His shadows coiled around him, fueling her fire but also somehow protecting his skin from the burns.

Her flames intensified as Rom entered her again and again, their bodies finding a rhythm together. He drove into her without mercy, his hands pinning her in place, his kisses hard and bruising. She felt him along every inch of her, his touch just as scorching as her own fire. His mouth found her breast and sucked, and she cried out his name. She felt a low hiss burn within her and knew her hair had transformed into snakes. She kept her eyes closed, riding the wave of pleasure with each stroke of his, with each movement of his body against hers.

He filled her again and again, stretching her wider and wider. His arm circled around her, cupping her ass and angling her so he could drive even deeper. Her legs clenched around him, tightening with need. The tension within her built and coiled, and it was all she could do to keep from melting into a puddle right then and there. Release shattered through her, and her vision blurred, stars igniting in her eyes, her flames skyrocketing, shooting into the sky like fireworks.

"Yes," Rom urged. "Gods, yes, Mare." He moaned, still pushing into her again and again until his own release shuddered through him.

But then something else followed. A heavy *crack* sounded between them, followed by a clap of thunder.

Magic ricocheted between them, white-hot and searing. Marina's body tensed, and Rom swore. They clung to each other, refusing to break apart despite the strange energy churning between them.

"I've got you, Mare," he said.

"What the hell is happening?" Marina shrieked.

Rom buried his face into her shoulder, and Marina held him close against her, trying to summon her fire to protect them from the onslaught of power coursing between them.

Rom unleashed a terrible scream of agony, his voice piercing through the night.

"Rom!" Marina cried, desperate to open her eyes, to see if he was all right. But she couldn't risk turning him to stone, not when Medusa's powers were still consuming her.

"It—It—I'm fine," Rom said, his tone lilting with surprise. The white light between them faded, leaving nothing but the darkness of midnight and the campfire beside them.

Slowly, they sat up, their bodies still entwined. Both of them were shivering, but not from the cold. Energy crackled and sizzled along Marina's flesh, and she felt her flames receding. Her head felt lighter as the snakes vanished from her scalp. Her eyes flew open as she looked at Rom, then gasped.

His flesh was unmarked, leaving nothing but

smooth, tan skin. The inky tattoos were completely gone. Her gaze roved over his naked body, searching for even an inch of the death magic on him.

But nothing was there. His body was free.

The curse was broken.

CHAPTER TWENTY-TWO

Marina, still breathless and overheated from their intercourse, could only gape at Rom as her sluggish mind struggled to keep up. All she managed to say was a single word: "How?"

Rom lifted his hands in front of him, turning them over slowly as he appraised his unmarred skin. "Gods above... I don't understand." He stared at her with wide eyes. "Was it your Gorgon magic?"

Marina frowned as she considered this. She had never exploded like that before. Perhaps the strength of it had burned the curse from his body entirely.

But something else crept into the corners of her mind... *Back to the beginning.*

Their curse had begun with the joining of their bodies in Tethys's sacred temple. And from the begin-

"

ning, Marina's touch had been a temporary cure for Rom's curse. The more she touched him—and the deeper that touch went—the less effect his curse had on him.

It only made sense that the most intense touches imaginable—the joining of their bodies once more—would be the ultimate cure for both of them.

"Tethys didn't curse you," Marina whispered. "She only wanted to keep you from returning to me. Because she used our lovemaking to fuel the curse, knowing it could never happen again."

Rom's brow furrowed, an incredulous look passing over his face. "Are you saying... that *sex* was the key to unlocking the curse?" He raised a doubtful eyebrow at her. "I mean, we were *good*, Mare, but even that's a stretch."

"Don't you see? Dahlia told me there was a key to unlocking every curse. That magic had to be bound a certain way. Tethys used our connection as the key to her curse. It was powerful magic, Rom. She couldn't do it alone; she had to tether that magic between us. And when we joined together in the most intense way possible..."

"It strengthened our magic and pushed out Tethys's," Rom said slowly. His eyes met hers in stunned realization. "Marina, when I asked you to burn..."

Marina nodded. "If I hadn't unleashed Medusa, it's

possible the curse wouldn't have been broken. But because I did..."

"We joined our magic together, *including* Medusa's powers. Holy gods..." Rom ran a hand along his face, then huffed a laugh of disbelief. "You did it, Mare. You really did it."

Marina leaned closer to him and pressed a gentle kiss to his lips. "*We* did it," she clarified.

Rom grinned and drew in for another kiss, this one longer and deeper, his tongue sweeping over her lower lip. Marina let herself sink into his embrace, relishing the solid, warm feel of his arms around her—and the knowledge that he wouldn't be turned to stone because of her.

Never again.

Marina was full of hope when she woke the next morning, still wrapped in Rom's arms. After digging through their packs for spare clothes—since their previous outfits had been torn in their haste to get naked the night before—they quickly dressed before setting off.

They continued their trek up the mountain in companionable silence, occasionally exchanging intimate smiles as they both reflected on their passionate night together. Marina marveled at this bond flowing freely between them. He wouldn't vanish like before, never to be seen again. This wasn't just one night they shared together, like at Litha. They would have many, many more nights to spend with one another, exploring each other's bodies and sealing their connection.

He was hers. And she was his.

The thought circled through her mind again and again, and she couldn't keep a smile from spreading across her face.

Rom was alive. And he was with her. Together, they could face anything.

They were ready for Tethys.

Pausing occasionally so Marina could summon her Gorgon magic and steer them in the right direction, they continued their journey, stopping only for meals, water breaks, and the occasional need to relieve themselves.

The sun had almost set when Marina felt the shift in the air. She stiffened, inhaling deeply and closing her eyes. In her mind, she saw the two women, chained to the cave wall, bruised and bloodied from the kelpies' torment. She could hear their cries. Smell their fear.

A burst of ice-cold magic speared through her—the same sensation she'd felt just before she'd faced Tethys in the woods.

The water goddess was nearby.

"We're close," she muttered.

"Are you sure we shouldn't stop for the night?" Rom asked, glancing toward the sun.

Marina shook her head. "We can't. I can *feel* them, Rom. We have to keep moving."

Rom nodded, letting her take the lead. Her steps quickened, her breaths turning into sharp pants, urgency flooding her veins. The harsh bite of Tethys's cold magic intensified inside her, chilling her to the bone. They were so close. *So close...*

"Mare!" Rom cried out.

But Marina was so focused on the path at her feet that she didn't see the kelpie appear in front of her, its huge body made of rocks and boulders. It reared its head back, slamming into her and knocking her backward. She tumbled down the gravel path, her body scraping against dirt and rocks. Rom shouted after her, but darkness pressed in on her, threatening to consume her.

Fire, she thought, and her body erupted in flames. The pain from her fall vanished, and Medusa's power roared to life. Shadows swelled around her, feeding her flames, as Rom conjured his death magic. With a feral screech, she lunged for the kelpie, striking it across the chest with her fire. It reared back with a high-pitched whine, but Marina wasn't finished. She struck again and again, carving holes into the beast's body until it disintegrated into a pile of pebbles at her feet.

Marina surged forward, rounding a corner and

approaching a cave she recognized from her mental journey with Medusa's spirit.

"This is it," she breathed, her steps slowing. Inside the cave was a dark abyss, waiting for them like the jaws of death.

Chains clinked, echoing in the vast space, and a raspy voice whispered, "Sister? Is that you?"

Marina's heart lurched. She almost sprinted toward the sound, but Rom grabbed her wrist, shaking his head in warning.

"We don't know what's waiting for us in there," he murmured. "Be careful."

Marina was torn between assuring him she'd be fine and jerking out of his grip. She felt invincible, but she knew that with her curse broken, she was more vulnerable.

Goddess, Marina could *die*. The finality of that thought momentarily shook her, freezing her in place. Marina hadn't been mortal in fifty years. This day, this moment, could finally be her undoing. Even with the Gorgon powers flowing through her, she could still be killed.

And so could her Gorgon sisters.

Resolve pulsing through her, Marina stepped into the shadows, keeping Medusa's magic wrapped around her. Her eyes adjusted immediately, thanks to her serpent senses, and she made out the two figures of the other

Gorgon sisters chained to the wall. Between them stood a towering figure clutching a massive spear.

No, not a spear... A *trident.*

It wasn't Tethys who was waiting for her.

"Oh, shit," Rom muttered.

"I was wondering when I'd finally get to meet you, Marina," said a deep, rumbling voice.

The figure stepped forward, and Marina's entire body stiffened with recognition. Not from her own memories, but from Medusa's. This god, this vile man before her, had violated Medusa in the worst way imaginable, taking her body by force. In return, Medusa had been transformed into the Gorgon.

Some saw it as a curse. But with Medusa's memories, Marina knew the truth. Athena had given Medusa the power to turn any man to stone if they dared to cross her. She would never be helpless again.

A low growl built in her throat at the sight of this man who had started it all. The man who took what he wanted with no thought of the consequences.

The god of seas. Neptune himself.

CHAPTER TWENTY-THREE

His windswept white hair fell down to his chin. His tall, muscular body was adorned with golden armor, similar to the armor Tethys had worn when Marina had last seen her. The smirk on his handsome face only made her blood boil with rage. Her hands clenched into tight fists at her side.

"What are you doing here?" Rom asked, stepping forward so he stood alongside Marina.

Neptune's gaze cut to Rom, and his smirk widened. "A death god? A prince of Hell? Well, this is unexpected. What a delight." He grinned as if they were old friends reuniting.

"Where's Tethys?" Marina growled.

Neptune barked out a harsh laugh. "Tethys? She was working under *my* orders. She's insignificant. And she won't be troubling you any further. I gave her a simple task, and she failed me, so now she is suffering for it." He shrugged one shoulder in a clear dismissal. "She was my spokesperson, but she was too hotheaded for her own good. I'm taking over the task now."

"And what task is that, exactly?" Marina bit out, every inch of her taut with awareness, poised to strike. Within her, her snake raged, ready to lash out at him.

"Why, eliminating Hestia's mutants, of course. You snake shifters are an abomination that never should have been created in the first place."

"And what do you call your kelpies?" Marina snapped. "Are those not also an abomination, created by a forbidden magic?"

Neptune offered a cold smile. "It was only a retaliation. Once the fire witches are wiped from existence, I'll end the kelpies next. All will be as it should."

"Who are you to decide that?" Rom spat. "You think you can just end an entire race of witches because you believe they should be destroyed?"

Neptune only looked at him blankly. "Yes. Or... do you not understand the vastness of my power? I am a *god*, you pathetic boy. My power surpasses even that of your brother, the god of the Underworld." He lifted his trident and slammed it into the rocky ground. The walls of the cave began to quiver, and the two Gorgons chained to the wall whimpered, cowering from the shower of pebbles raining from the ceiling.

"Stop," Marina said, stepping forward. All it would take was a tendril of Neptune's power to bring the cave crashing down on all of them. And Marina wasn't sure if the other Gorgons were strong enough to survive it.

Marina's mind was spinning, her head still reeling from Neptune's presence. She'd expected to face off with Tethys, not *him*—the god of the seas. Tethys had been a difficult enough opponent, but Neptune? Could he even be killed?

Think fast, Marina told herself. *You have to find the other fire witches. Farah, Wren, Dahlia... Find them, and they can fight with you.*

She tucked her hands behind her back, summoning a ball of fire and focusing on the coven of witches she'd come to love. Her finger swirled in the air, and a coil of flame darted away from her, vanishing into the darkness as it sought out her fellow fire witches.

Find them, she urged her magic.

Neptune's eyes narrowed on her, and she blurted out the first thing that came to her mind: "Why?"

He frowned. "Why what?"

"Why did you assault Medusa? Why wage war on Hestia? Why do *any* of this?" She gestured to the cave in its entirety. "Surely you have better things to do than attack those weaker than you."

Neptune's frown deepened. "I punish those who defy me, as all gods do. This reckoning was a long time coming, little witch. Those who cross me must be destroyed."

"*Cross you*?" Marina repeated. "How, exactly, did Medusa cross you? By not consenting to sharing a bed with you?"

Neptune's face twisted into a snarl. "You know *nothing*, foul witch."

"I know *everything*." Marina took a step forward, seething with rage. "I have Medusa's soul—and her memories. I know everything that happened between you two. Her magic flows through my veins."

"You may have Medusa's essence, but your powers are nothing against mine," Neptune sneered. "You and your fire witches will be destroyed soon enough."

"Why? Why even keep them alive?" Marina couldn't help but ask him. She had to know.

"Why kill them when I can turn them into slaves to do my work for me?" Neptune's face split into a wide, malicious grin. "There is something truly empowering about watching my enemies kneel before me."

Rage burned in Marina's chest, igniting her fire. But she had to contain it. She didn't know where the fire witches were yet.

As if summoned, her fire magic returned to her, showing her a brief vision of the other witches. They were chained up, deeper within the cave. She couldn't get to them without passing by Neptune.

She couldn't kill him, not with one strike. She would need to make the blow count if she hoped to get past him. Her eyes cut to Rom, who was staring at her. She widened her eyes before she jerked her head subtly toward Neptune.

Rom inclined his head ever so slightly. He understood what she was asking.

Goddess, she hoped this wasn't a death sentence for him. If she broke his curse only for him to get himself killed, she'd never forgive herself.

Marina spread her arms, offering a sarcastic smile to Neptune. "Well, I'm here now. Go ahead and destroy me. What are you waiting for?"

Neptune's expression hardened. "With the spirit of Medusa residing in you, I must banish her first, lest she inhabit another witch and continue her vendetta against me."

Vendetta. As if Neptune were blameless. As if *he* hadn't started this war in the first place by violating Medusa.

But this explained why he'd kept the Gorgon sisters alive. He wanted to banish their spirits, too.

"Fine." Marina lifted her chin. "Do your worst, Neptune. Try to banish her."

Neptune's eyebrows lowered as he scrutinized her, clearly suspicious.

Marina forced a laugh. "What's the problem? Are you afraid of her? I wouldn't blame you."

Neptune snarled and took a step toward her. His grip momentarily slackened on his trident, offering Marina the opening she needed. "I am not—"

She didn't let him finish. With a shout, Marina lunged, sending a ball of fire straight into Neptune's chest. He went down, and Rom's shadows came next, swirling around the sea god like a dark tornado, obscuring him from view.

"Go!" Rom shouted.

Marina darted forward, dodging Neptune's shadowy form and ignoring his roar of fury as she surged deeper into the cave. Neptune's cries intensified as Rom continued to assault him with his death magic.

But it wouldn't hold him off for long.

Fire burned in Marina's veins, urging her onward, showing her the way. She trusted it, following where it led, winding through tunnels and caverns until she heard the distinct clang of chains echoing around her.

"Marina!" rasped a voice.

Farah noticed her first, her hair a matted mess around her face, her eyes bloodshot. She sat up straighter against the cave wall, her arms straining against the chains. "How did you find us?"

"No time," Marina muttered. She pressed a hand to the chain links binding Farah to the wall. Fire poured from her fingers, melting the metal until it snapped and fell to the ground. "Can you access your magic?"

Farah groaned as she rose to her feet. "No. My powers are spent. My serpent needs to be unleashed before I can summon."

Damn. Marina was on her own.

Farah touched her arm. "I'm glad to see you, Marina, but I wish you hadn't come. This war is so much bigger than we feared."

"I know. I've already met Neptune."

Farah's face paled. "How—"

The ground shook, and Marina swore as she almost lost her balance. She glanced up at the cavern ceiling as rocks fell from above.

She was out of time.

With careful steps, she darted from witch to witch, melting their chains and freeing them. Some were already shifting to their serpent forms when she finished. The ground shook again, and Farah shouted her name.

Marina spun around, her heart jolting in her chest. Neptune stood at the mouth of the cave, fury etched into his face. His golden eyes surveyed the serpents and witches around him, and he laughed coldly.

"You think this makes a difference? You think your

pitiful coven of witches can match *my* power?" His voice rose in volume, and he raised his trident in the air. The ground rumbled, and the sound of rushing water filled Marina's ears.

Oh, shit. Marina tensed, her body filled with panic as water flooded the cave, churning and roiling like the river she'd grown up with.

Marina sent a burst of fire toward Neptune, but he was undeterred, twisting his trident in the air. Several kelpies rose out of the water, streaking toward the witches with their high-pitched whinnies.

"No!" Marina screamed as one of the witches shrieked, backing away as the kelpies cornered her.

"Marina!" Farah cried out, dodging a strike from another kelpie. "Free the other Gorgons! We'll hold him off. *Go!*"

Marina turned to Neptune, who advanced, his face darkening with fury. He aimed his trident at Marina, who ducked just before a burst of white sparks shot toward her, searing the top of her head. She straightened, unleashing Medusa's rage. Her body shifted, rising in height until she towered over Neptune, whose eyes widened in surprise.

Yes. Let him fear her. Let him see the true extent of her power. She refused to be cowed by him.

Marina struck, her snakes lashing toward Neptune. He staggered back a step with a grunt, but one snake managed to strike him in the neck. Silver blood droplets oozed from the wound.

With a roar of fury, Neptune slashed his trident in the air, and a burst of ice-cold magic sliced into Marina's chest, momentarily quenching her flames. Neptune pushed onward, taking advantage of her lapse in power. He struck with his trident again and again, sending shards of ice into Marina's flesh, pinning her against the cave wall. Pain lanced through her, brutal and merciless. Coldness crept into her veins, making her shiver and dousing her fire. She tried to summon it back, but the chill bit into her, fierce and unyielding, stronger than even her flames.

She couldn't get past it. She couldn't get past *him*. He was too strong.

Strong enough to overcome Rom. Had he killed him? Marina didn't want to think of it...

Neptune suddenly cried out in pain, and Marina's gaze snapped to him. Several serpents glided forward in the water that still gushed freely into the cave. Their fangs gleamed as they surged toward the sea god. Every single witch had shifted to her serpent form, slithering forward to assault Neptune.

All so Marina could escape. This was for *her*.

One of the cobras turned its head to look at Marina, and she recognized the gold pattern on its scales. Farah. The look in her amber eyes seemed to say, *Go now!*

Marina thrashed against the shards of ice still pinning her to the wall. Blood poured down her arms, mingling with the spray of water. The cave was slowly filling, and if she remained here much longer, she would drown. A scream tore from her throat as she managed to pull one arm free. Hot blood gushed from her wounds, but she pushed aside the pain and used her free hand to tug the icicles from her body. With a grunt, she fell into the water, the cuts stinging from the icy chill of it. The serpents were twined around Neptune's body as they struck again and again. A flash of white light, and one of the snakes fell, its lifeless body floating in the water.

Horror burned in Marina's chest, but she swam forward, ducking behind Neptune. Goddess, he would kill those witches one at a time...

But Marina could save them. She could save all of them. She just had to free her sisters first.

Her movements were slowed by her blood loss as she waded through the water, cursing Neptune and his damned ocean for slowing her down. Pain blurred her vision, but she pushed herself onward, grateful for Medusa's towering form that allowed her to swim faster than a normal human.

But it still wasn't fast enough. Darkness crept into her eyes, threatening to consume her. She wouldn't last much longer.

"Mare!" a voice cried.

Marina halted, inhaling a shuddering gasp of relief. Thank the Goddess. Rom was alive! "Rom! I'm coming!"

Spurred by the sound of his voice, Marina swam faster, pushing past the waves lapping toward her as she made her way back to the cave entrance.

When she finally reached it, she found Rom with a bloody gash on his scalp, dripping silver blood. Remembering whose power she wielded, she averted her gaze and warned, "Look away, Rom!"

"Don't worry, I'm not looking at you." He stood alongside one of the Gorgons—the one with the shaved head—as he struggled to undo her chains. With a hiss of pain, he drew back, cradling his hand, which had crimson, pus-filled bubbles spreading along his skin.

"It's bewitched against god blood," Rom said with a groan, turning his hand over. "I can't touch it."

God blood. Marina had Hestia's blood in her veins. It would be immune to her as well.

But she had to try.

She sent a burst of flame straight into the chains, but nothing happened. It remained intact, impervious to her powers.

"Only water magic... can free us," choked the Gorgon, her hooded eyes fixed on Marina.

Water magic. Shit. The only one with water magic was Neptune. "Rom?" she asked, hoping he had a solution.

But he just shook his head slowly. "My shadows don't work on it, either."

Marina curled her hands into fists and let out a shout of frustration. She was *so close*. There had to be a way... There had to...

The magic is all around us. It lives in the water at our feet. It lives in the rivers and the seas.

Remy's voice echoed in her mind, and Marina swallowed down a lump of emotion. She hadn't allowed herself to think of Remy since she'd learned the entire coven had meant to kill her.

But it was Remy's words that would save them now.

It wasn't just ordinary water flowing at their feet. It was enchanted water. *Neptune's* water.

Marina crouched down cupping her hands together to gather as many water droplets as she could. With dripping fingers, she lifted the water to the chains and summoned her fire. Steam rose from her hands, but the water trickled along the chains, sizzling from the impact. Neptune's magic scorched her skin, and she bit down hard on her lip as pain bloomed along her palms. But she kept pouring the water on the chains, gritting her teeth through the agony until the chains snapped, and the Gorgon dropped into the water.

Marina groaned, examining the blistering boils along her skin. But there wasn't time. She ducked down low, helping the Gorgon to her feet, before the two of them sloshed through the water to reach the other sister. With help, Marina was able to break the chains with minimal damage to her other palm, though a few boils sprang to life along her skin. Together, she and the first Gorgon helped the second to her feet.

"I'm Marina," Marina said, pressing a hand to her chest.

"Vivian," said the woman with the shaved head.

"Lilith," said the other, smiling gratefully at Marina. "Thank you, Marina. For reuniting us at last."

Vivian glanced between them. "Are you ready?"

Marina and Lilith nodded. Water poured around them, trickling down the slick cave walls. The chill of Neptune's power pressed in on Marina, icing her bones and making her shiver.

The three sisters joined hands, and when their skin touched, warmth spread through Marina, burning away Neptune's magic and melting the ice that had collected in her chest. She sighed with relief and said, "This is it. Rom, get down."

He ducked, plunging his head underwater. Marina clenched her sisters' hands, pain burning from the boils on her skin. As one, they channeled the power of the Gorgons.

And fire exploded around them.

CHAPTER TWENTY-FOUR

FIRE ROARED AROUND THEM AS MEDUSA'S MAGIC overwhelmed Marina's body, healing her injuries and igniting her powers. The flames rose in height until they reached the ceiling, and before long, Neptune's river evaporated. Steam surrounded the Gorgon sisters as they channeled their powers.

Beside her, Vivian and Lilith shifted, their bodies growing in height. Serpents sprang from their scalps, hissing and spitting. Their eyes flashed an intense gold, spearing right through Marina as she looked into them. She was unaffected by the poison in those eyes, but she could still feel the lethal power burning from them. The gold in their eyes scorched with an otherworldly glow, seeing right into Marina's soul. Their skin shimmered like starlight, and she understood now why Rom had called her beautiful. The Gorgon sisters were like statues come to life, but instead of being made of stone, it was like they were cut from diamonds.

Beautiful indeed.

Together, the three sisters unleashed an unholy scream that reverberated off the cave walls, making the ground rumble. As one, they moved, gliding through the tunnels with inhuman speed. Within seconds, they reached the cavern where Neptune continued to fight off the serpents. Marina's heart twisted at the sight of so many dead snakes lying in the water.

No more. No more blood would be shed for this war.

It would end today.

The three Gorgons shrieked again, and the walls quivered.

Neptune froze, whirling to face them, his face stricken with terror. Marina delighted in that expression, the way his face paled like a petrified human.

He was nothing. *Nothing* compared to their power.

Their hands still clasped, the three sisters surged toward him, their snakes lashing out for him. Their gold eyes flashed as they burned into Neptune's gaze, and he screamed, his pitiful wail echoing in the vast chamber. The three Gorgons surrounded him, allowing him no escape as their flames burned into him, rising higher and higher. His screams intensified, and a loud *clang* reverberated along the walls as his trident fell to the ground.

Marina pushed her flames onward, urging her snakes to assault him again and again. The Gorgons continued to scream with their fury as they poured their power into the attack, merciless and relentless.

Neptune fell to his knees, covering his ears, which were bleeding. And still, the Gorgons screamed. By now, the last remaining snakes had fled the scene, for which Marina was grateful; she didn't want any of the witches to suffer while they ended Neptune's life.

"Please!" Neptune cried out.

But the Gorgons ignored his pleas, just as he'd ignored Medusa's. They speared their power straight into his chest, and silver blood spurted from the impact. With one final cry, Neptune sank into the water, bubbles rising from his descent.

He did not rise again.

Slowly, the waters stopped flowing, and the flames from the Gorgons dried it up. Neptune's body was nowhere to be found, but Marina knew deep within her that he was dead.

Marina released her sisters' hands with a gasp, her body suddenly drained. She shrank back down to her normal height, releasing Medusa's energy and sagging against the cave wall. Vivian and Lilith did the same, panting from exertion. They were still bruised and bleeding from Neptune's imprisonment, but their faces were alight with relief and triumph.

"Thank you," Marina murmured. "I couldn't have done this without you."

Vivian surged forward, wrapping her in a tight embrace. "You saved us, Marina. We owe you our lives."

Marina's throat filled with emotion as Lilith joined in their embrace, the three of them clinging to each other tightly. Though Marina had only just met them, her heart swelled with familiarity. Her soul knew theirs. They were kindred spirits.

Sisters. Family.

Marina's eyes burned with the knowledge that she had friends and loved ones for the first time in her life. Remy would always be her mother, but Marina had never truly belonged to that coven. Even if they had spared her life.

But here and now, with the Gorgons and the fire witches around her, Marina was finally at home.

Over Lilith's shoulder, she caught sight of Rom lingering in the cave entrance, a small smile on his face. His head injury was still bleeding, but he otherwise looked unharmed. Marina gazed at him, trying to convey everything she felt—the gratitude, the love, the exquisite affection she had for him—into that single gaze.

Rom's eyes heated as he returned that look before giving her a nod of approval.

When the sisters finally withdrew, Marina approached him and clutched his face in both her hands. "You were magnificent," she whispered before kissing him full on the mouth.

He returned her kiss before groaning in pain. He raised a hand to the wound in his head and winced. "Neptune dealt me a heavy blow earlier. This will take a while to heal."

"But you're alive," Marina said, stroking the back of his neck. "That's what matters."

Rom's eyes turned somber. "The same can't be said for the fire witches."

A lump formed in Marina's throat as she turned to look at the fallen serpents behind her. She counted six of them. Six witches who would never rise, who would never wield Hestia's magic again. Six who had died... for her. Her eyes roved over each serpent, some she recognized and some she didn't. Her heart twisted with part relief and part agony as she realized Dahlia, Farah, and Wren were not among the dead. She knew their serpent forms well enough.

But six souls had been lost today in Neptune's ruthless war against Hestia's chosen people. Not to mention the countless other fire witches who had been hunted and killed over the years.

But today, it was over. Today, they were free.

"Marina!"

Marina turned and saw Farah racing toward her. They met in a tight embrace, arms circling each other as they both sighed in relief. Behind her were Dahlia, Wren, and the remaining fire witches, all sustaining injuries. But they were still here. Alive. Marina embraced each of them as they all dissolved into tearful exclamations of gratitude. Even Rom was dragged forward as several witches wrapped their arms around him, kissing his cheeks and forehead enough to make him blush.

Marina wasn't sure how long they remained in the cave. Perhaps hours. Perhaps days. But with Neptune and the kelpies gone, it didn't matter. They were *free*. They could live in these caves if they wanted to.

This didn't mean they were no longer in danger; the entire realm still saw fire witches as an abomination, and that certainly wouldn't change overnight. Tethys was also still out there somewhere. She was licking her wounds now, but she would likely retaliate, even without Neptune commanding her.

And, worst of all, the Gorgons had killed Neptune, the mighty sea god. There would certainly be repercussions for this from the other gods and goddesses of Elysium.

But for now, the war against Hestia had finally ended. The kelpies would no longer hunt them. They could live freely once more.

When they finally exited the cave, Marina appeared at Rom's side, her arm linking with his. He squeezed her tightly against him, his gaze tender as he looked at her. Together, they emerged into the sunlight, squinting against the brightness.

"I must say," Farah said from behind Marina, "we have never welcomed a man into our coven before." Her eyes turned to Rom and softened slightly. "But we would gladly welcome you, Romanos, if you would care to join us."

Rom's eyebrows lifted in surprise, but instead of responding, he turned to Marina. "I go where she goes."

Warmth blossomed in Marina's chest, and she leaned in to brush her lips against his. When she withdrew, she found Farah eyeing them with a smirk on her face.

"We'd be delighted to join your coven," Marina said. She scanned the crowd of witches until her eyes fell on Vivian and Lilith, who were watching the interaction with interest. "And you, my sisters? Where will you go?"

Vivian and Lilith exchanged glances before the former responded, "We will reside with your coven for a short time. But there is much of the world we hope to see."

Marina nodded. She'd been alive for over fifty years, but the same couldn't be said for her sisters. She didn't know how long Neptune had imprisoned them, and she could hardly blame them for wanting to see more of the world.

They would always be sisters. And they would always be able to find one another.

Still arm in arm with Rom, Marina descended the mountain with the other witches, her chest blooming with triumph and the promise of a better future.

Want another romance like Marina and Rom's? Read Ivy & Bone, a Hades and Persephone retelling with a twist, featuring Rom's brother, Cyrus!

LEARN MORE AT RLPEREZ.COM/IVY-AND-BONE

ABOUT THE AUTHOR

R.L. Perez is an author, wife, mother, reader, writer, and teacher. She lives in Florida with her husband and three kids. On a regular basis, she can usually be found napping, reading, feverishly writing, revising, or watching an abundance of Netflix. More than anything, she loves spending time with her family. Her greatest joys are her children, nature, literature, and chocolate.

Subscribe to her newsletter for new releases, promotions, giveaways, and book recommendations! Get a FREE eBook when you sign up at subscribe.rlperez.com.